D0060463

By Danielle Steel

SECOND ACT • HAPPINESS • PALAZZO • THE WEDDING PLANNER
WORTHY OPPONENTS • WITHOUT A TRACE • THE WHITTIERS
THE HIGH NOTES • THE CHALLENGE • SUSPECTS • BEAUTIFUL
HIGH STAKES • INVISIBLE • FLYING ANGELS • THE BUTLER
COMPLICATIONS • NINE LIVES • FINDING ASHLEY • THE AFFAIR
NEIGHBORS • ALL THAT GLITTERS • ROYAL • DADDY'S GIRLS
THE WEDDING DRESS • THE NUMBERS GAME • MORAL COMPASS
SPY • CHILD'S PLAY • THE DARK SIDE • LOST AND FOUND
BLESSING IN DISGUISE • SILENT NIGHT • TURNING POINT
BEAUCHAMP HALL • IN HIS FATHER'S FOOTSTEPS • THE GOOD FIGHT
THE CAST • ACCIDENTAL HEROES • FALL FROM GRACE
PAST PERFECT • FAIRYTALE • THE RIGHT TIME • THE DUCHESS
AGAINST ALL ODDS • DANGEROUS GAMES • THE MISTRESS
THE AWARD • RUSHING WATERS • MAGIC • THE APARTMENT
PROPERTY OF A NOBLEWOMAN • BLUE • PRECIOUS GIFTS
UNDERCOVER • COUNTRY • PRODIGAL SON • PEGASUS
A PERFECT LIFE • POWER PLAY • WINNERS • FIRST SIGHT
UNTIL THE END OF TIME • THE SINS OF THE MOTHER
FRIENDS FOREVER • BETRAYAL • HOTEL VENDÔME
HAPPY BIRTHDAY • 44 CHARLES STREET • LEGACY • FAMILY TIES
BIG GIRL • SOUTHERN LIGHTS • MATTERS OF THE HEART
ONE DAY AT A TIME • A GOOD WOMAN • ROGUE • HONOR THYSELF
AMAZING GRACE • BUNGALOW 2 • SISTERS • H.R.H. • COMING OUT
THE HOUSE • TOXIC BACHELORS • MIRACLE • IMPOSSIBLE ECHOES
SECOND CHANCE • RANSOM • SAFE HARBOUR • JOHNNY ANGEL
DATING GAME • ANSWERED PRAYERS • SUNSET IN ST. TROPEZ
THE COTTAGE • THE KISS • LEAP OF FAITH • LONE EAGLE • JOURNEY
THE HOUSE ON HOPE STREET • THE WEDDING
IRRESISTIBLE FORCES • GRANNY DAN • BITTERSWEET
MIRROR IMAGE • THE KLONE AND I • THE LONG ROAD HOME
THE GHOST • SPECIAL DELIVERY • THE RANCH • SILENT HONOR
MALICE • FIVE DAYS IN PARIS • LIGHTNING • WINGS • THE GIFT
ACCIDENT • VANISHED • MIXED BLESSINGS • JEWELS • NO GREATER
LOVE • HEARTBEAT • MESSAGE FROM NAM • DADDY • STAR • ZOYA
KALEIDOSCOPE • FINE THINGS • WANDERLUST • SECRETS
FAMILY ALBUM • FULL CIRCLE • CHANGES • THURSTON HOUS
CROSSINGS • ONCE IN A LIFETIME • A PERFECT STRANGER
REMEMBRANCE • PALOMINO • LOVE: *POEMS* • THE RING • LOVING
TO LOVE AGAIN • SUMMER'S END • SEASON OF PASSION
THE PROMISE • NOW AND FOREVER • PASSION'S PROMISE
GOING HOME

Nonfiction
PURE JOY: *The Dogs We Love*
A GIFT OF HOPE: *Helping the Homeless*
HIS BRIGHT LIGHT: *The Story of Nick Traina*

For Children
PRETTY MINNIE IN PARIS
PRETTY MINNIE IN HOLLYWOOD

WITHOUT A TRACE

DANIELLE STEEL

WITHOUT A TRACE

A Novel

Dell
New York

2023 Dell Mass Market Edition

Copyright © 2023 by Danielle Steel
Excerpt from *The Ball at Versailles* by Danielle Steel
copyright © 2023 by Danielle Steel

Published in the United States by Dell,
an imprint of Random House, a division of
Penguin Random House LLC, New York.

Dell and the D colophon are registered trademarks of
Penguin Random House LLC.

Originally published in hardcover in the United States by
Delacorte Press, an imprint of Random House, a division
of Penguin Random House LLC, in 2023.

This book contains an excerpt from the forthcoming book
The Ball at Versailles by Danielle Steel. This excerpt has
been set for this edition only and may not reflect the
final content of the forthcoming edition.

ISBN 978-1-9848-2188-1
Ebook ISBN 978-1-9848-2187-4

Cover design: Mimi Bark
Cover image: © Moslem Sheihaky/500px/Getty Images

Printed in the United States of America

randomhousebooks.com

2 4 6 8 9 7 5 3 1

Dell mass market edition: November 2023

To my brave, beloved,
wonderful children,
Beatie, Trevor, Todd, Nick,
Samantha, Victoria, Vanessa,
Maxx, and Zara,

May you always be safe and wise
and well loved,
and brave enough to correct
your mistakes when you need to,
and change course.

May your love run smoothly,
and joy and peace fill your days.

May you be forever blessed.

I love you,
Mom / d.s.

WITHOUT A TRACE

Chapter 1

Charles Vincent had been sitting in his office in Paris waiting to talk to his boss for more than two hours. It was Friday afternoon and he had promised his wife Isabelle that he'd leave the city early. He had a three-hour drive ahead of him, the last half on narrow, rough country roads along the coast of Normandy. They had houseguests at their château that weekend, friends of Isabelle's, although he knew them too. He worked late so often, and traveled so much for work, that she had a fully developed social life without him. He didn't mind. They had a wide circle of friends. She had her own, as well as a group of devoted women friends whose husbands worked as hard as Charlie, or were divorced, so Isabelle never lacked for company when Charlie was busy. She didn't mind going to events or entertaining without him, but he had promised to be there that night. It was someone's birthday, the husband of one of her friends. Isabelle had organized a weekend around them at the château. She was proud of their country home on a hill overlooking the rugged coastline and the sea. The château was beautiful. They had owned it for ten years.

Charles was the CEO of the biggest plastics manufacturer in France, Jansen Plastics. It was his second career, a reincarnation after an earlier life. The job at Jansen had saved him eleven years ago.

He was waiting to meet with the owner and founder, Jerome Jansen, eighty-two years old and still going strong. Jansen's only son had moved to the States years before to seek his fortune, had married an American, and had no interest in the business, nor in coming back to France, or stepping into his father's shoes. He was a U.S. citizen now, as were his wife and kids. France was ancient history to him. When his son had finally made that clear to him, after he made his own fortune in the fast food business in Los Angeles and Southern California, Jerome Jansen had set out to find a CEO who could help him run his business with intelligence and an iron hand.

Jerome Jansen owned the largest toy company in France, along with factories that made plastic products for other uses. It was a huge operation, and Charlie's path had crossed with Jansen's at the right time. Charlie's father had been a writer of considerable literary acclaim in France but only modest commercial success, which had indirectly led Charlie into the publishing business right after college. He loved books and everything related to them except writing. His meteoric rise had been astonishing and impressive, and he found he loved the business. He had no talent for writing himself, and had struggled all his life for his father's approval as an only son, which had been hard-earned and of short duration. Although proud of him, and stern, Charlie's father had died two years after Charlie started working in publishing. His father's wishes had been hard to live up to. His mother had been kinder and died when he was very young, and his father was a hard taskmaster. Driven and hardworking, Charlie had been educated in the best French schools. He loved his job and everything about it, except for Gilles Vermier, the tyrant who owned the business. He made Charlie's life a living hell for all sixteen years he worked there. His consistent victories in spite of his boss won him the reputation of the golden boy of the publishing world. Although the publishing house had an impressive stable of authors before he arrived, Charlie had successfully lured both French and foreign writers of major reputation, and enhanced the house he worked for immeasurably. His forward-thinking instincts led them into digital books before anyone else. He used the American market as his model to try to add audiobooks to their list before any other publisher in France. He had a gift for marketing, and understood writers and their quirks, thanks to his own difficult father.

Within five years after he was hired, Charlie had a glowing reputation in publishing, and within ten he was a star. The owner of the house knew it, resented him personally, and fought Charlie on every improvement he wanted to make. Instead of giving up, Charlie fought harder for what he knew would sell. The owner's only son had died in an accident, and Charlie became the golden boy of his business, bringing it into the future, and making it the greatest publishing house in France. His boss grudgingly acknowledged it, but disliked Charlie personally. Charlie often felt that Vermier bitterly held it against him because he was vital and alive, and his own son had died so young.

In the end, a point of honor unraveled Charlie's career, as fast as his meteoric rise had catapulted him into publishing stardom before that. A small argument became a big one. It was about adding soft porn to their list for purely commercial reasons. The owner was for it, and Charlie opposed. The owner's massive ego was challenged, and he hired an outsider over Charlie to control him, and force Charlie to endorse their position. What ensued were two years of battles, followed by a massive showdown, and a situation Charlie could no longer tolerate. They slowly squeezed him into a corner, and he had to either swallow his pride and give into them, or leave. He opted for the latter, after a bloody war. He quit in a blaze of pride and fury, and with the absolute certainty that he'd have no trouble finding a job he liked better, with a more reasonable owner at the helm, with values similar to his own.

He quit two weeks before his fortieth birthday, and he rapidly discovered that he was no longer viewed as the golden boy of publishing. His constant battles with the owner and the owner's new hire had tarnished Charlie's reputation. He knocked on every door in publishing, and found that he was considered "difficult," and no one wanted to hire him. He had risen too high, had been paid too well, had used his own ego and principles to achieve autonomy, and had followed his own lead. It was a humbling and very hard lesson for him. He had assumed too much, and couldn't land a new job.

The publishing house where he had worked promoted someone from the internal ranks to take his place, make fewer waves, and do exactly what the owner wanted with no resistance. They opened a whole category of soft porn, which didn't do as well as they'd hoped and had been sure it would. The business suffered as a result, and several of the big authors he had brought to them left when Charlie did, but for two years Charlie was out of a job. His world crumbled around him, and his personal life went with it.

Isabelle, his wife, was fun and lively and spirited when they were young and just out of college. She had studied art history and was bright and well educated. She was from a respected family, attended the best French schools, worked briefly at the Louvre, chose not to work once they were married, and stayed home to raise their children. She had no real career ambitions. She took care of their son Olivier, and six years later Judith. Isabelle's father owned several of the biggest luxury brands in France, a champagne label, high-end leather goods, and jewelry lines, all extremely profitable businesses. She had been brought up not for a career, but instead groomed to be the wife of a very successful man, someone like her father. She was used to the perks that went with first a father's and then a husband's success. She entertained lavishly, was fashionably elegant, intelligent, and the perfect wife for a head of industry, not for a failure, which was what Charlie became overnight. She made it clear to him every single day after he quit his job in publishing that she expected him to get back on top again, immediately.

Charlie had been brought up to respect and achieve intellectual excellence, and his writer father was puzzled by his interest in "commerce." Charlie's mother had died when he was in college. She had been a gentle woman, a college professor at the Sorbonne and a poet laureate. None of that meant anything to Isabelle. She was familiar with her father's relatively ruthless success. Her three sisters had married prominent men, but none as successful as Charlie had been for sixteen years, and she was proud to be his wife then, and infinitely less so once he was unemployed.

Her father had seen the makings of greatness in Charlie in his youth, but after sixteen years in publishing, and two after that without a job, he told his daughter that the fire in Charlie's belly had gone out. Charlie knew it too. He didn't want to do battle anymore. He wanted a simpler job and a better life. He didn't want to have to put himself on the line every day, like a commando, fighting wars he couldn't win against unreasonable men with massive egos, who held all the cards. He was never going to be as successful as Isabelle's father. Fighting for what he believed was right, on principle, he had burned his bridges in the publishing world. With his reputation for being stubborn, too independent, and difficult, he couldn't find a single job in publishing for two long years, even in a lesser position. He was overqualified for every job he applied for, and unable to get hired.

Charlie had gotten desperate. He had dipped heavily into his savings, and Isabelle had borrowed money from her father, which she considered the ultimate humiliation. So did Charlie, although he had paid back every penny when he was employed again. But he was tainted in Isabelle's mind by then, and she could never feel the same way about him afterwards. He was a marked man for her from then on. She couldn't respect him, or even share a bed with him. Their marriage was as dead as his career.

Materially, Jerome Jansen had turned everything around for him. He was looking for an exceptional CEO for his business, since his son was successful in LA. He had heard about Charlie from a mutual friend, who had used Charlie as an example of what can happen when you reach the top, make a bold move out of pride and ego, and can't find another high-level job in your field. Charlie had been out of work for just over two years by then, and although the friend didn't know it, Isabelle had just given him an ultimatum: find a job immediately or she wanted a divorce. The two years of humiliation being married to him was more than she could bear. Borrowing from her father had been the last straw. They couldn't even afford to pay for Judith's private school, or for Olivier to attend the private university where he had been accepted and was about to enter. Isabelle's father paid for that as well, yet another humiliation for Charlie. Isabelle had pointed out that he couldn't even pay for his children's education, and she was too ashamed to see her friends. Charlie had been living in a haze of increasing despair for two years when Jerome Jansen called him. The mutual friend had vouched for him, said that Charlie was brilliant. Jansen was hesitant, since Charlie had never been in industry, but the friend had convinced Jerome that it was the man at the top that made a difference, not the product he was selling. He felt sure that Charlie could make the transition from his experience in publishing. Jansen's business was in a slump at the time, and he wanted to do something drastic to take the lead over his competitors. He met with Charlie twice, and saw exactly what their mutual friend saw in him. Even in a somewhat subdued state, Charlie had something special about him. He was smart, creative, and resourceful. He knew nothing whatsoever about plastics then, and he was sure that Isabelle would think it was beneath her, but when she heard the salary Jerome Jansen was offering, she reconsidered. She was impressed by the bonuses Charlie could make if he could improve their profits significantly, and beat out their competitors. And Charlie was intrigued by the challenge of learning something new, and eager to try. The prospect brought him back to life.

Charlie studied the plastics business intensely, and learned everything there was to know about the toy industry. He came back to Jansen with a wealth of exciting, innovative ideas. Jansen increased his offer, and Charlie took the job. Within a few years he had made good on his promises, and so had his employer. They were the leaders in the toy industry, a highly lucrative business, and every home in France with a child in it had a mountain of Jansen toys. Within five years, their entire plastics business had grown to astronomical proportions. They were the leaders in the plastics industry across the board. Eleven years after he was hired, Charlie was one of the most influential businessmen in France. What he had made in publishing seemed paltry by comparison. He was a rich man now, in a respected position. He didn't love it as he had publishing, but it was no longer a question for him of having a job in a field he loved, it was about being able to support his family, and leave them something significant one day, and about keeping his marriage together.

Although he was still handsome, with dark hair and brown eyes, the feelings between him and Isabelle weren't warm, and hadn't been in years. He had worked for Jerome Jansen for eleven years, and he had earned every penny he'd made there. Jansen was more agreeable to work for than Gilles Vermier, his previous boss and the owner of the publishing company, had been. Jansen was just as resistant to change and new ideas, but he was smart enough to listen to Charlie in most cases, and knew that Charlie had his finger on the pulse of their industry and had infallible instincts. Jansen was just as given to cheap, sometimes sleazy solutions and ideas as the owner had been in publishing. He had wanted to introduce a line of sex toys under another brand name that Charlie had fought him on relentlessly. No one would buy their children's toys if they found out the company was also making sex toys. Children's toys were their biggest moneymaker. Jerome Jansen had listened to Charlie about that, but not about other things.

Jerome hated putting safety warnings on toys, which he was convinced would reduce sales. They were obliged by law to include certain warnings, but Jerome put no more on them than he had to. He thought the warnings were unsightly and put a negative spin on the appeal of the toy. Charlie insisted on adding them even when not imposed by law. He wanted every child who used their toys to be safe. Jansen rarely saw his grandchildren in LA and wasn't fond of children in general. He really didn't care about the well-being and safety of their customers' children. He just wanted their parents' money. Jerome was a businessman, not a family man. Charlie was more interested in averting tragedy, even if there was an ugly sticker on a doll or a toy, or if every pool toy came with a warning. Charlie had a heart and a conscience. Jerome Jansen didn't. Isabelle wasn't much better. She loved the lifestyle Jansen Plastics had given her. She really didn't care what they produced. Her motives were entirely transparent as to why she was still married to Charlie. He had delivered on his promises to her, and had risen to the top again. It was all she cared about, being the envy of her friends, and having unlimited money to spend on whatever she wanted.

A year after Charlie had gone to work for Jerome, and they had repaid Isabelle's father, Charlie had bought Isabelle a château on the Normandy coast, three hours outside Paris. It was in poor condition, and they had remodeled it for a year, to all of Isabelle's specifications. The project became her obsession. The location was superb, on a small cliff, looking far out to sea, on a rugged shoreline. They turned it into Isabelle's dream of luxury and comfort. He had bought it to thank her for staying married to him through the hard times. She often thought that if she had divorced him a few months sooner, when she wanted to, she would have missed out on the château he'd given her. It had been worth staying married for, but it didn't warm or revive her feelings for him. She had lost respect for and interest in him during his two years of unemployment. She had hated being married to a failure. In her mind her own prestige depended on his success. She had lost all hope of his recovering from it, and making something of himself again. He had proven her wrong, and justified Jerome Jansen's faith in him. She also knew that Charlie didn't love his job, and that dealing with his boss was an agony for him most of the time. He stayed in the job because he didn't dare risk another two years lost in the desert, with a dry spell like the one he'd been through before. He had no choice but to stay in his current job if he wanted Isabelle to remain his wife. He knew she would have left him the instant he quit. The thought never even crossed his mind. At fifty-three, he knew that this was his fate for the rest of his career.

At twenty-nine, his son Olivier was independent now and had a good job in London. Judith, at twenty-three, had only recently finished her studies and had her first job in New York. She often sought his advice. She was a graduate of the prestigious Ecole Hôtelière in Switzerland. And Isabelle had a standard to maintain, to show the world that she was married to a winner, not a loser. She would never have tolerated a humiliation like that again. She was fifty- two, a year younger than Charlie, but their two years of poverty had marked her in deeper ways and instilled a fear in her of losing what she cherished most: her lifestyle, more than the person who provided it. She had something to show for her thirty years of marriage, a splendid fully remodeled château, in glorious condition, full of art, antiques, and objects of great value, and an apartment in Paris, on the ultrafashionable Champ de Mars in the 7th Arrondissement, with a perfect view of the Eiffel Tower which everyone envied. She had all the status symbols she wanted. She liked being the object of envy, not of pity. She had found that soul-crushing when it happened to her. Her job was being married to Charlie, even if she didn't enjoy his company. They no longer had anything in common, and all semblance of love or desire had left them years before. Their relationship and love for each other had died and vanished along the way. It no longer mattered when, it just had. She spent most of her time with her friends, shopping, and enjoying fancy lunches with them, and spa weeks, all at his expense. Providing that for her was what was expected of him. He fully understood that now, that what he gave her materially was all that mattered to her, not the human being he was. And he was willing to do whatever he had to, to preserve his marriage. He believed that marriage was forever and commitments were to be honored. He found solace in books, as he always had, and in his passion for vintage cars.

He also knew that whatever disagreements he had with Jerome, about his policies or his lack of concern about the safety of the children who used their toys, which was essential to Charlie and not to Jerome, he was as married to Jerome as he was to Isabelle. The two went hand in hand. They owned him. He was trapped, by the salary he made, and the astounding bonuses Jansen paid him every year, as the success of the company continued to skyrocket, thanks to Charlie's vision and gift for business.

Isabelle was like a human calculator. She knew exactly how much he made at all times. She spent it lavishly, and told Charlie that she did it all for him, the exquisite décor, the beauty of their homes, even the chic clothes she wore. She said she did it all to improve Charlie's image, just as Jerome acted as though what he paid Charlie was a philanthropic gesture, when in fact, it was blood money he paid to Charlie to stay in his job. So far it had always worked. Charlie had never refused to do what Jerome expected of him, nor what his wife did. He was a man of his word. The echo of Isabelle threatening to divorce him eleven years before still rang in his ears. He would do what he had to for the rest of his life, and stay in the job at Jansen Plastics. He got one pass in his lifetime, to be a failure and out of work for two years. He wouldn't have dared to risk that again. Isabelle wouldn't have tolerated it.

It was twenty after seven at night when Jerome finally appeared in Charlie's office. He was waiting patiently at his desk, answering emails and texts. There was no hope now of getting to the château in time for the dinner party that night, or even the birthday cake afterwards. Isabelle was used to his having to stay late at work, at Jerome's whim, and didn't care.

They dined formally at dinner at the château during their weekend parties, and there was no way now that he'd even make it there for dessert. They would have to manage without him, which Isabelle did extremely well. Charlie wondered what excuse she'd give, probably just that he was busy and had stayed late for a meeting, which was usually true. He was never in a rush to get home. Sometimes he actually dawdled on purpose on Friday afternoons, so he could arrive at the château late enough to miss the dinner and festivities she organized nearly every weekend for her friends.

There was no joy for him in those evenings, only duty. His life was ruled by Isabelle's ever-increasing expectations of him, and Jerome Jansen's arguments to bring him into line. Jerome enjoyed it. He always had to "win." Isabelle and Jerome both owned Charlie, in different ways, for different reasons, although the financial result was much the same, and benefited both of them, more than it did Charlie. The money Charlie earned just passed through his hands briefly, on its way to pay for Isabelle's follies. In effect, although he never expressed it that way, he was their hostage. Jerome's because he had given Charlie the second career that had saved him, a far more lucrative one than he'd had before, though in a field he hated and didn't care about. And he was Isabelle's hostage because if he didn't maintain the high standard she felt was her due, he knew that she would leave the marriage this time, and their children, even though adults now, would be devastated, or so she claimed. And Charlie loved his children more than anything. He knew they were comfortable with the illusion that their parents had a solid marriage, and he never told them the truth, that it was only as solid as the funds he brought home to support it. One slip, and it would be all over. He and Isabelle stayed together now out of duty, habit, and tradition, and he be-

lieved in all three. He couldn't even remember
when he had stopped loving her, or she him, even
long before he had left publishing. They had lost
the spirit and life of their union somewhere along
the way, it probably didn't even matter when. It
was what it was now, and Charlie had no illusions
about it. He felt like a robot at times, and had lost
his zest for life. His life was all about duty. He was
always working, ever more successful, and rarely
saw his old friends anymore, or pursued the pas-
times he used to enjoy. He had had more fun when
he was younger. He was rich now, but not happy.

He liked the château, but it didn't mean to him
what it did to Isabelle. She needed it for her status.
He liked it on winter days when the weather was
bad and the sky gray, and he could go on long soli-
tary walks. He felt at home there then. On the
weekends of her house parties, it felt to him like
someone else's house and he had landed there by
mistake. He felt like an unwelcome stranger. The
château belonged to Isabelle, since he gave it to
her, to thank her after two frightening years, for
staying married to him. What she did there, and
who she entertained, was entirely up to her. She
never consulted him about it, nor about anything.
She was an independent woman who had found
her voice and her legs in middle age, particularly
once her children had grown up and left home. At
fifty-two, she was in full control of everything that
mattered to her. He was never quite sure he mat-

tered to her, but he knew enough not to ask difficult questions. She never seemed to miss her
children, although Charlie had missed them acutely
once they moved away, and he still did.

Charlie and Isabelle rolled along like two paral-
lel lines. They intersected occasionally, but never at
a deep level. It was the road map of his life now,
and what he knew his future would look like, weekends at the château, weekdays in their city apartment. She took trips with her women friends, and
he traveled for business. It was his only opportunity for occasional infidelities. They didn't happen
often, and had never been meaningful. He had
never fallen in love with anyone else. He had become accustomed to a loveless existence. He couldn't
even remember what love felt like, or having a job
that truly mattered to him. He did what was expected, what he had committed to do. He was an
honorable man who did what he promised, and
had for his entire life, except for his one daring moment when he had walked out on his publishing
job and had been punished severely for it. He knew
better now, although working for Jerome Jansen
was never a pleasure, no matter how much money
he made. He had sold his soul to keep Isabelle
happy, and he, Jerome, and Isabelle all knew it.
Even his father-in-law had been pleased and approved when he took the job in plastics. He had
said it was what good men did to honor their marriage. Charlie no longer had young children to pro-

tect, but he had an institution to uphold, and appearances he respected.

When Jerome walked into Charlie's office on Friday night, he looked disgruntled. Charlie was fairly certain it was about a new set of stickers Charlie had ordered to have printed and applied to an entire line of toys, with safety warnings for the parents.

"They look like shit. What's the point of telling them their kids can break their necks, or an arm or a leg? Why not just put a sticker on the box, telling them 'Don't Buy This Toy.'" He was angry at Charlie, who looked unfazed by the comment. He'd heard it all before. It was a recurring argument between them.

"That's always an option. You don't want someone getting hurt, Jerome. Think of the lawsuits that would result." Charlie knew a lawsuit would concern him, not the safety of a child. They were different-sized trampolines, which kids of all ages loved, but they had considerable risks if not properly supervised.

"They'll sue us anyway, even with your damn stickers. I want you to cancel the stickers."

"That wouldn't be wise, Jerry. And you know it." Charlie remained outwardly calm, respectful, and polite, as always.

"Then make them smaller and put them under-neath the product where parents won't see them."

"That defeats the purpose. I don't want to wait to do it until after someone gets hurt, and if you think about it, neither do you. Imagine some little girl paralyzed because her older brother let her use his trampoline." The thought horrified Charlie but not Jerome.

"We're not babysitters, we're toy manufacturers. It's the parents' job to watch out for their kids, not ours," he said cavalierly.

"It's our job to wake the parents up and remind them of that, and that some toys could be danger-ous," Charlie insisted.

"I'm giving you till Monday to recall the product and get your damn sticker off before we put it on the market." Threats usually worked for Jerry, with everyone but Charlie, who knew how to reason with him. Charlie usually won the argument, but Jerry needed to drag him in the dirt first. And, when he absolutely had to, Charlie gave in. Not this time. The issue was too important. They were within government guidelines, but Charlie wanted to go farther than that with this particular product. It was too potentially dangerous not to. The stakes were just too high for them not to go the extra mile with a more explicit warning.

"I'm not recalling the stickers, Jerry," Charlie said firmly.

"You'll do what I goddamn tell you to. Don't forget who owns this place. My name is on the front of the building, not yours. I call the shots here!" Jerry shouted at him, which made younger employees cringe. Charlie knew him better than that and how to handle him.

"You pay me to give you sound marketing and merchandising advice. Don't make it a waste of money. You need to listen to good sense here," Charlie said seriously.

"Don't tell me what to do!" Jerry shouted at him, stormed out, and slammed the door to Charlie's office. Charlie closed his eyes for a minute, trying to keep his composure. For the first time in eleven years, he was tempted to do what he'd done before, and march straight into the owner's office, quit, and walk out. But then what would he do? He knew what that looked like now. At fifty-three, there would be no jobs comparable to this one at the very top of the heap, even more so now than when he was forty. Thirteen years later, if he quit in a rage, it might be his last job forever, and he wasn't ready to face that. He knew what Isabelle's reaction would be. She would call her father's attorney about a divorce the next morning. Charlie had money saved, but there was never enough to support her lifestyle for long. He needed to keep working for many years to come. How much was enough? He had never been able to determine that number. It was always more than he thought, because of some new luxury she couldn't live without.

He got up to leave then. It was eight o'clock. He had a three-hour drive ahead of him, or longer in weekend traffic. He thought about stopping to get something to eat on the road, but after Jerry's shouting at him at the top of his lungs, he wasn't hungry. He could eat the leftovers from the dinner party when he got to the château. And he had had a big business lunch. He could have used a drink too, but not before driving on the long, winding last half of the road to the château. He would have liked to storm into Jerry's office and quit before he left, but he knew better. He was fully an adult. He didn't have the right to quit just because it would feel good to do it in the moment. The severity of the consequences just wasn't worth it, no matter how it ate at his soul to deal with Jerry.

Charlie was tired when he got in his car in the parking garage, underneath the Jansen Plastics offices, in an industrial part of Paris, in the 11th Arrondissement. His parking space was marked CEO. He drove a small compact car, instead of something fancier. It was better suited to getting around crowded Paris streets than bigger cars were. Isabelle drove a Mercedes. He didn't like showy, expensive cars, although he dreamed of having an Aston Martin one day, maybe when he retired, whenever that would be. He thought of buying one to restore it but didn't have time.

He followed the traffic out of the city. It was heavy at that hour. People were still leaving work, an hour after most offices closed. He got a text from Isabelle once he was on the road, telling him to come in the morning if he was too tired to drive that night, since he would miss the dinner party anyway. He didn't bother to answer. She'd see him when he arrived. He was lost in his own thoughts, thinking about Jerry and the scene in his office, and Jerry's orders to get the warning stickers off the trampolines. He was tired of the battles with Jerry, tired of all of it. Maybe he'd feel better on Monday, but for now he felt like a schoolboy who had been scolded by his father or the headmaster. His father had been stern with him when he was a boy, and unfair at times, and as an only child, all his father's hopes and expectations had rested on him, and he had tried to live up to them. Now Isabelle's did, and his children's, and Jerry's. They all expected a lot of him. It was a heavy mantle to wear at times.

Charlie was still a handsome man, even in his fifties. He had dark hair with only a little gray at the temples, and warm brown eyes. There was an air of kindness to him, which enhanced his good looks. He was tall, athletic, and in good shape, although his wife no longer noticed or cared what he looked like.

It was an easy trip until halfway there, and then he had to leave the highway at Étretat and took the smaller local roads, which followed the coast and wound around hairpin turns, taking him danger-ously close to the edge of the enormous cliffs along the coast. Some were a hundred feet high, others smaller. There were always spots along the road with heaps of flowers and makeshift crosses where unwary drivers had gone over the edge of the cliff and fallen to their deaths on the rocks below. See-ing the flowers of homemade memorials was al-ways a good reminder.

The ocean shimmered in the moonlight on a warm June night, and he relaxed finally, basking in the beauty of the scene and the drive. The château was grander than he liked, although it suited Isa-belle perfectly. What he liked best was the road there, and the peace he felt while driving. He loved driving there alone, and usually did. It calmed him after a long day. Isabelle drove herself earlier, in the afternoon. She left after lunch and was there by the late afternoon. He drove at night and loved it.

He could feel his whole body relax, as he took the familiar hairpin turns. It was one of the few places he could challenge his driving skill as the car hugged the road, and for an instant he felt like a racecar driver. It had been his dream as a child to be one. He had always loved cars and still did, and knew a lot about them. He loved going to car shows.

He was smiling on the deserted road. There were no houses nearby and long distances of nothing but the dark road, the cliffs, which got smaller, and the sea crashing on the rocks below them. With the window open, he could hear it. There were miles between houses on that part of the trip, which made it even more peaceful.

As he took another turn, going a little faster than usual, his eyelids fluttered closed, and he could feel the car start to slide and dreamed that he was on a racetrack. He was still smiling as the car slid over the edge of the road, with nothing to stop it, and plunged thirty feet down the rock face of the cliff. He woke up sharply, and realized what was happening. He had gone right over the edge of the road, down the cliff, and the car was pointing toward the rocks below. There was nothing he could do to stop it. The car banged and scraped along the cliff on the way down, jarring him sharply. It took only seconds, but felt like years, as the car continued its trajectory down, and in the light of the full moon, he could see clearly the rocks and the spray from the ocean below him. He felt his whole body go limp. There was nothing he could fight or stop or change. He hit his head and barely noticed. A jutting rock hit the driver's door hinges hard and the door tore open. His seatbelt kept him from falling out. He knew that he was facing his certain death, and felt an enormous wave of peace wash over him. He didn't even mind dying. There was nothing left to do. He knew his life was over, as the car hit the rocks and flipped into the sea. He had never expected dying would be this easy. He wasn't afraid. He was relieved. It was over.

Chapter 2

Charlie woke as though from a dream, as the car bounced off the rocks, fell into the water, and went under. He felt paralyzed for an instant, and then instinct took over. With the door open on the driver's side, the car filled with water in seconds. He had his seatbelt off, and was out of the car just as it slid down further in the water. He had seen movies of people struggling to get out of submerged cars and drowning in them. But with the door badly damaged and wide open he was able to swim free of it before the car sank deeper. He swam underwater, as the car went deeper down, and managed to swim away from it. He felt like he was underwater for a long time, pulled by the currents, and then with his lungs feeling like they were bursting, he exploded to the surface and tried to swim with the currents. They kept him from going far and

pushed him toward the rocks, and when he got
close enough, he reached out and grabbed them,
and held on tightly, as the rough rock surface tore
at his hands, which he didn't even notice. He had
an instant of thinking that if he let go now, he
would drown and that might not be a bad thing.
And then survival took over. He found a foothold,
and clambered onto a rock at the base of the cliff.
He lay there for a long time, with the spray of the
sea soaking him with each wave. He clung there
until he caught his breath and looked further along
the cliff, at the path he had come, not far away,
straight down onto the rocks and into the water. He
couldn't believe he was alive, and for a moment he
was almost disappointed. His clothes were soaked,
his jacket was gone, his shirt was torn, and the
lace-up shoes he wore to the office were still on,
which made it slippery and hard to negotiate the
rocks, but allowed him to crawl across them without cutting his feet. The jagged rocks tore his trousers.

He sat looking at the cliff face, and could see
places where he could climb once he had the
strength to do so. He wondered again if it would
just be easier to let himself slip back into the sea
and drown. It was almost tempting, and very appealing. He had been ready to die only minutes before. But he was cold and wet, and he thought he
could make it up the cliff face if he didn't fall and
die. It was a chance to survive, if he wanted to. He

didn't think about it, he just did it. He made his way gingerly across the rocks, clutching onto boulders, and reached the base of the cliff, where he saw a little natural shelf to stand on. He took a leap to get there, and found hand- and footholds all the way up the cliff, as though providence had wanted him to meet the challenge to live and had helped him. The decision was made for him.

He had no idea how long it took him to get back up the cliff or what time it was. His watch was gone. When he got to the top of the cliff, he rolled onto the ground and found himself lying on the road. He lay there for a long time, wondering how many others had survived the drop to the rocks below. Judging by the flowers he had seen along the road so many times, surely not many. He wasn't sorry now that he'd lived, but mostly surprised he had, and had wanted to.

His legs felt shaky when he finally stood up. It didn't feel like he had broken any bones, and he was able to walk, although his hands and legs were bloody. When he touched his face, he could tell it was scraped and bleeding too. It didn't hurt, he felt numb. Not knowing what else to do, he started walking down the road, with no idea where the next house was. He couldn't remember seeing any for miles. He walked in the direction he'd been driving, going toward the château. It had been a good hour and a half's drive farther when he'd gone over the cliff. He felt as though the fall, the time in the water, and climbing back up had taken hours, but he had no clear concept of time as he walked slowly down the road, without seeing a house or a car.

His legs felt weak from time to time, and he sat down on a log or a rock, rested, and then continued on the road. He felt like he'd been walking for hours but realized it was probably just an hour or so. Then he felt as though he couldn't go another step. He went off the road into a little clearing of trees, thinking he would look for a grassy area or some leaves to sleep on and would keep going in the morning. He could go no further now, and had been pushed beyond his endurance. His cell phone had vanished with the car.

As he stepped off the road, he saw some lights through the trees coming from what looked like a cabin. He headed toward it, stumbling over rough terrain, through grass and bushes, and then saw a narrow dirt driveway off to his left. His legs felt like rubber by the time he got to the house and knocked on the door. He could see lights within, but heard no sound in the cabin. No one answered, and he knocked again. Finally he heard footsteps, and a woman's voice. He felt almost about to faint.

"Yes, who is it?" she said, sounding stern. It was late by then.

"I'm sorry . . . I . . . I need help . . . I've had an accident." His voice was weak. She hesitated, and then cautiously opened the door, and gasped when she saw him. His face was scraped and covered in blood, as were his arms and hands from climbing the cliff. His shirt was torn and in shreds. He felt no pain and she thought he looked as though he was in shock. His pants were ripped and there was blood on them too. She opened the door for him to come in. He stepped inside on shaking legs.

"Oh my God, what happened?" She led him into the kitchen, and pulled out a chair for him. He sat down heavily, and the room swam around him. He looked very pale. She went to get him a glass of water and handed it to him.

"I'm sorry to intrude," he said, leaning back in the chair. "I need to use your phone." He had no idea what time it was. It felt like the middle of the night. He saw a clock that said midnight. He noticed an easel with a painting on it. The woman was wearing a man's shirt splattered with paint, and jeans equally so. She was beautiful, with long blond hair and green eyes, and looked at him apologetically.

"I don't have a phone. And my cell phone is broken. I keep meaning to get a new one. I don't really need one here. I can drive you into the village tomorrow to get one or make a call. Where did you leave your car? Did someone hit you, or did you hit a tree?"

"I went over the cliff. It must have been a couple of hours ago, around ten. I fell asleep. The car went down in the sea." She couldn't believe that he'd survived, and neither could he. She started running clean towels under the cold water, and gently wiped his face. The scrapes were full of grit and debris. He sat there without moving, feeling like he was in some kind of surreal dream. He felt no pain, and had a sensation of floating as she cleaned his face.

"How did you get back up the cliff?" she asked him.

"I'm not sure . . . I climbed. There were enough hand- and footholds to get me back to the road. And then I walked here."

"It's a miracle that you survived, and didn't fall off the cliff." And it was a bigger one that he hadn't drowned when the car fell into the sea. She continued cleaning his injuries as he looked at her. She left the room and came back with bandages, and helped him pull off the remains of his torn shirt, and then his trousers after he removed his wet, badly scraped shoes. He was getting stiff, and he looked exhausted. He could barely talk. "There isn't a hospital near here, but I can drive you to one in Le Havre if you like," she offered.

"I'm not sure I could stand up again." He smiled at her and then winced, as she cleaned the cuts on his arms, which were deeper, and the nasty scrapes on his palms. She brought him one of the old men's shirts she used for painting, which fit him, and she came back with paint-splattered overalls that looked big enough to fit him and must have been huge on her. She was tall and very thin. She covered him with a towel and cleaned the cuts on his legs. She could tell from the well-cut dark hair and the shoes that he must have looked respectable before he went over the cliff and nearly drowned at sea.

He wondered if Isabelle was worried about him by then, or if she was still busy with her guests, and just assumed that he was late. There was no way for him to call her from here, and he was too tired and shaken to go anywhere. None of his wounds needed stitches. They were mostly very ugly scrapes, filled with dirt and gravel. The ones on his palms were the worst, from his climb up the cliff. He had just kept going and never felt the pain.

"I have a house up the road from here, an hour and a half away, near Veules-les-Roses," he explained, and started to shake. She put a blanket around his shoulders, and he looked a sorry sight as she sat down across from him, and saw the wedding band on his finger.

"Do you want something to eat? Are you hungry?" He shook his head, almost too tired to talk by then. "You should sleep."

"My name is Charles Vincent," he said.

"Aude Saint-Martin." She went to get bedding and made him a bed on the couch. "We should get you to the hospital tomorrow, to make sure nothing is broken."

"I don't think it is. I walked a long way down the

road to get here. I think I must have hit my head, but I seem to have come out of it okay." He smiled and she shook her head and smiled at him.

"You're a miracle, you know." She had a gentle smile.

"I don't feel like one. I feel like I fell over a cliff," he said with a wry smile. She led him to the couch, and he lay down gratefully, put his head on the pillow, and pulled up the blanket she had given him. He could barely keep his eyes open as she turned off the light, and he lay there thinking about her after she went back to the kitchen. She was obviously an artist, and he wondered what she was doing in this rustic cabin all alone. She hadn't hesitated to take him in once she saw that he was injured. He could hear her moving around the kitchen, which was comforting. He felt peaceful and safe and still stunned to be alive. He was exhausted, and drifted off to sleep with the distant sounds of her in the kitchen, putting away the first-aid supplies.

She tried to be quiet as he slept on the couch and she sat in the kitchen, thinking about what he'd been through and how incredible it was that he'd survived. She was wide awake herself after the adrenaline rush of tending to him and trying to assess if he needed professional medical attention. But surprisingly, although his superficial cuts and scrapes were bad ones, he had come through it amazingly unscathed, given the fact that he'd driven off a cliff, hit the rocks below, and nearly drowned. And it was a long drop down. Clearly his time hadn't come and he had been spared.

She listened for him and heard no sound. Around three A.M., on her way to her bedroom, she tiptoed past him and stopped to look at him closely. She could see that he was breathing, and he gave a start and his eyes fluttered open. He stared at her and then smiled as he recognized her.

"I keep dreaming that I'm falling," he whispered, noticing again how beautiful she was in the moonlight that bathed the room. Her face looked delicately sculpted with fine features.

"I think that's a memory, not a dream," she said softly, wondering if he'd have nightmares for a while. It wouldn't be surprising after what he'd been through. "Go back to sleep." She spoke as she would have to a child. She tucked him in securely and he let her. He liked knowing she was there with him. It was reassuring.

"I keep thinking of when the car went over the side, I was heading toward the rocks and knew I was going to die, but I wasn't afraid, and now I'm here. It's all so surreal. I'm sorry if I scared you." He was whispering too.

"You didn't. I'm not afraid to be here alone," she said. "Your wife will be worried about you," she said, and he didn't answer for a minute.

"No, she won't." His voice was a little stronger. He was fully awake now. "She probably thinks I de-

cided not to drive up till the morning. I had an argument with my boss," he said vaguely, and she
listened quietly, and sat down on the couch, next to
him. He felt oddly safe and at ease with her, as
though he had entered a different universe, almost
as though he had died and was now a ghost. It was
an eerie feeling, like an out-of-body experience.
His mind felt separate from his body.

"What did you argue with him about?" She was
curious about him, who he was, and where he
came from. It was as if he'd fallen out of the sky
and appeared on her doorstep.

"We argued about a product we're making,
which could be dangerous for children. We make
toys. I used to be a publisher," he said, his mind
rambling from subject to subject, as she listened. "I
liked that better, working with writers and books.
My father was a writer."

"Why did you stop being a publisher?"

"I had an argument with that boss too."

She smiled. "You have arguments with a lot of
people." He thought about it. They were still speaking softly but not whispering.

"Maybe I do. I run the companies and they own
them. Sometimes I don't agree with what they
want to do." It was a simple way to explain it and
it was true. He looked tired after he explained it to
her. It took some effort.

"Do you like your job?" she asked him gently,
and he shook his head, honest with her.

"No, I don't. For a minute when I knew the car was going to hit the water, I didn't mind that I was going to die. I felt peaceful about it, and then the car went under the water, and I swam out. I guess I wasn't ready to die after all." He sounded surprised as he said it, and a little disappointed. She felt sad for him that he had been so willing to die, even for a minute. It didn't speak well for his life.

"I'm glad you didn't die," she said softly. She didn't know him, but he seemed like a nice person, and he had kind eyes. She didn't ask him about his wife, it felt too intrusive. His admitting that he'd been willing to die seemed more important. She touched his hand gently and he looked at her. They didn't speak for a few minutes.

"I'm glad I didn't die too," he said softly finally. "I feel like a ghost. I could have been dead by now." The thought didn't scare him, it surprised him. He had no fear of death now. He had come so close.

"I'm sure a lot of people would be very sad if you died," she said, and he looked pensive.

"I'm not sure that's true. It would be inconvenient for them if I died, but that's not the same thing as being sad. There are people who depend on me."

"Do you have children?" she asked him. They were whispering in the dark. He didn't notice when he took her hand in his and held it, despite his bandaged palms. It felt so natural to do it, to be here with her, talking. It felt like the right place to be at that exact moment, with the woman who had cleaned and bandaged his wounds and nursed him so gently. She was like an angel ministering to him, a total stranger.

"I have a son and a daughter. My son is in London, my daughter is in New York. They're grown up. They don't need me now. I'm not sure anyone really does. Maybe that's why I felt peaceful when I thought I was going to die, but I still swam out of the car, and climbed back up the cliff. I suppose that says something about my will to live."

"You're not going to die for a long time," she said, and he reached up and touched her face softly. He was too big for the bed she had made him on the couch. "Come on," she said in a soft voice. "You're too tall for the couch." His feet were hanging off. She grabbed the blanket and helped him up. When he stood, he seemed stiff but firmer on his feet than before. She took him by the hand and led him to her bedroom. "I changed the sheets this morning, I haven't slept in them yet," she said as she helped him slip between the cool clean sheets and tucked him in.

"Where are you going to sleep?" he asked her, looking anxious.

"On the couch." She smiled. She started to leave the room and he grabbed her hand.

"Don't leave," his eyes pleaded with her. He didn't want to say it but he felt as though if he slept and was alone, he might die in the night. But if she was there with him, he knew he wouldn't. She was the Angel of Life, not the Angel of Death he had followed off the cliff into the sea.

She sat down on the bed next to him and he never took his eyes off her. She lay down on the blanket, her head on the pillow, and he rolled slowly toward her and kissed her. He didn't know what he was going to do, and it was still the dark of night, but it felt natural to both of them, even though they were strangers. He felt as though he wouldn't exist if she wasn't there with him. She was the thread that was connecting him to life, as thin as a spider web and as delicate. He had a sudden overpowering desire to make love to her, to embrace life and prove to both of them that he was alive. Death still seemed so close, and life so ephemeral and so precious.

She slipped out of her clothes, and under the covers with him. She was naked and not sure if they should be doing this, but she was suddenly as desperate as he was. They made love ever so gently, mindful of his injuries. She cradled him in her arms afterwards, and he fell into a deep sleep. She lay holding him for hours, not wanting to disturb him, and he woke in the bright sunlight in the morning and smiled at her. She had dozed on and off while she held him, always ready to wake up fully if he needed her. She felt as though he had been sent to her to care for him and lead him back to life.

The night before seemed so unreal, except that she seemed very real as she lay naked next to him. More real than anything or anyone else in his life.

"I feel as though I know you, Aude," he whispered to her, feeling peaceful. They lay close together and she held him, as though to protect him and keep him safe. They both wanted to remember this moment and the night before forever. It was magical. She knew he couldn't stay. He had a life to go back to. But for now, for this one moment in their lives, they belonged to each other. It seemed very simple and clean and honest. It was the moment of his rebirth, of his coming back to life, and deciding to live. She made him glad that he was alive. He hadn't felt that way in years. It was as though he'd had to almost die to feel alive again. It felt like a dream to both of them. It was as though she had entered his dream with him the night before when they made love.

He had never met anyone like her. She seemed so free, living alone in her cabin with her paintings, her beautiful body lying next to him, infusing her own life into him. She gave him strength. He looked at her long, graceful body beside him, and they made love again. Afterwards, she helped him up, left him at the bathroom, and went to make him breakfast. He followed her to the kitchen a few minutes later to watch her. He had put on the shirt and overalls she'd given him, and she had put on a bathrobe, but now he knew every inch of what was under it, the exquisite silk of her skin and the wonders of her body.

She put bacon and eggs down in front of him and the food smelled delicious. She drank a cup of coffee and watched him. Everything seemed suddenly different, the sounds and smells, all the colors were more vibrant as he looked around.

"I'll drive you into town when things open so you can make your phone call," she told him after breakfast. She put the dishes in the sink as he smiled at her.

"Last night seems like a dream. I hope it was real," he said softly.

"So do I." But she didn't see how it could be.

"Is there a garage where I can rent some kind of car to drive home?" She had to remind herself that he belonged to others now, and not to her. He had belonged to her the night before and never would again. It made each moment they had more precious. They would have another hour or two together, and then he would leave and she would never see him again. But they would both remember their night forever.

"There's a garage. The owner, Armand, can lend you a car to drive home," she said quietly. She didn't offer to drive him, knowing it wouldn't be appropriate for her to enter his world. He had to leave her here, and go back where he belonged. It was why she had made love with him the night before.

He saw his face in the bathroom mirror after breakfast when he went to shower and was shocked at how bad he looked. He had bruises, cuts, and scrapes all over his face and dark circles under his eyes. But there was a peaceful look in his eyes that hadn't been there before, of wisdom and even joy. He had faced his own death and somehow survived it. "I look like a monster," he said, embarrassed.

"No, you look like a man who drove over a cliff into the ocean and nearly drowned. You're very lucky," she reminded him, and he nodded. He was grateful now to be alive and be here with her. He hadn't felt gratitude in a long time either.

They showered together and dressed slowly, savoring each moment, watching each other, knowing their time was running out, like sand in an hourglass. Their time together was limited. He put the shirt and overalls back on, and she dressed in jeans and a red sweater, and when she knew that everything would be open in the nearest village, Vattetot-sur-Mer, she drove him to it.

It looked to him like a little town of dollhouses. Everything seemed quaint and small and so peaceful here. They walked down the street together hand in hand. He knew he should report the accident to the police but didn't have the energy to do it. He said he'd do it by phone from home later. He remembered at the garage that he had no ID papers, and no money or credit cards. Aude loaned him the money to rent a car, an old, beat-up Renault the garage owner was working on. Armand knew Aude, and was comfortable letting Charlie have the car for a few days. He could tell Charlie was a serious, respectable person, despite the odd clothes he was wearing. Aude and Charlie stopped and bought him a shirt and jeans and running shoes, and he threw away his broken shoes. The soles had torn away from the leather. He gave her back the overalls and her painting shirt. They kept nothing to remember each other by.

And then he kissed Aude one last time, and got in the car outside the garage, as she watched him. He said he felt up to the drive when she asked him. He had another hour and a half left to the château, now that he knew where he was. He got in the car and waved, and she was sure she'd never see him again. But she had had one precious night with him, the night he survived. And she knew they would both remember it forever. He had his own life to go back to now, in a place where she couldn't go with him.

As she watched him go, tears slid down her cheeks as Armand watched her. He had never seen her with a man before, when she came in to get her car fixed. Then she got in her car and drove home. She climbed into bed, she could still smell him on her pillow. She wondered what kind of life he had gone back to. She knew he didn't like his job, or his boss, and he didn't think his wife would miss him if he died, but his children would, even though they lived far away. It sounded like a sad life to her, and she already missed him, a man she barely knew, who had walked into her life like a ghost. She had never done anything like it or known anyone like him. But she knew to the depths of her soul that what she had done was right, to open her heart to him, even for one night. The other thing she knew for certain was that she would never see him again, and would never forget him.

Chapter 3

The château was in a beautiful location, just over three hours out of Paris. There was another château, quite a famous one, in the vicinity, Château de Cany. It was about thirty minutes away from Charlie and Isabelle's château, which was near Veules-les-Roses, which had six hundred and fifty inhabitants, and was thought to be one of the prettiest villages in Normandy.

Isabelle was in the dining room with her guests, being served breakfast by the butler she hired when they had house parties on the weekends. She had a chef who came in to make meals for them. The food at the château was always excellent. She was known for it. They had a well-stocked wine cellar. Her closest woman friend, Stephanie Bonnard, was seated next to her. Stephanie had a keen wit, a sharp eye, and an even sharper tongue, and Isabelle always enjoyed her company. She could be honest with her, and the two of them were merciless when they talked about their friends. Isabelle was much closer to Stephanie than she was to her sisters, whom she found bourgeois and dull and saw very seldom. And Charlie had never particularly liked their husbands, whom he found dull and pompous.

By comparison, Stephanie was much racier, had been divorced twice, and had done well for herself financially. Her reputation had suffered somewhat in the last divorce. She had married a much older man with a great deal of money, and her intentions had been obvious. She gave Isabelle good advice about how to spend Charlie's money. The two women enjoyed traveling together, and did so often, to spas or fancy hotels in London, Rome, and Milan to go shopping.

"Did Charlie make it in last night at some ungodly hour?" Stephanie asked Isabelle as she sipped her coffee at breakfast, and Isabelle shrugged in answer, while the other guests chatted around the table. Isabelle had invited five couples for the weekend, with Stephanie the only single woman, and Edmond, an extremely polite, cultured, confirmed bachelor who added charm and elegance to any group. Stephanie sometimes used him as an escort, and had invited him. He was a reliable, very gracious houseguest, and hostesses were happy to have him. Isabelle had told Stephanie to bring him, although she knew that Charlie didn't like him. He thought he was a pretentious phony, and Edmond's charm was wasted on him. Charlie avoided him whenever possible, and he wasn't fond of Stephanie either. He thought she was a bad influence on Isabelle, and was a notorious gold digger, who was getting less and less attractive and more obvious as she got older. He was quite sure that if Isabelle didn't have his money and her father's fortune to inherit one day, Stephanie wouldn't have spent five minutes with her. She was a frequent and ready guest at the château. She and Charlie barely tolerated each other. They saw through each other. He knew her game, and she thought him a dullard with no backbone who probably cheated on Isabelle. She thought Isabelle could do a lot better, and always encouraged her to look around for new opportunities. Isabelle had done about as well as she was going to with Charlie, and the marriage had been dead for years. Stephanie thought she should look for someone older, and richer, possibly with a title to further her social career in loftier circles. Charlie had never provided her the social life Stephanie thought her friend deserved, and aspired to herself.

"He probably decided to stay in town last night, if the meeting went late," Isabelle said about her husband. "I texted him to stay in town if he was tired, but he never answered. He'll probably show up for lunch," she said casually, and Stephanie didn't comment. She was a short woman with sizable breast implants her first husband had paid for, and dyed hair a little too red, but she dressed well, and had impressive jewelry. She helped Isabelle pick the gifts she wanted Charlie to buy her for her birthdays and Christmas. Charlie saw her as a troublemaker, always encouraging Isabelle to be more extravagant. Isabelle was a previously natural blonde and still beautiful.

"Maybe he went out last night and he'll sleep late," Stephanie finally said, and Isabelle nodded. As long as he showed up in time for lunch she didn't care.

The whole group went for a walk after breakfast, and admired the gardens. Isabelle spent a great deal of time planning them, and she enjoyed her guests' compliments. Then they broke into smaller groups, sat in the chairs on the patio, and enjoyed the late spring sunshine. There was a good breeze from the sea, and the sky was bright blue. Four of the guests went to play tennis, and Isabelle went to discuss lunch with the cook. They were having lobster, and had had caviar the night before. Isabelle was just as glad that Charlie hadn't shown up to complain about it. He thought they spent too much money on their weekend guests. Isabelle had served them some of his best wines from their cellar, which would have annoyed him too.

* * *

Charlie still hadn't shown up when they sat down to lunch at one-thirty. Isabelle had called his cell phone twice and it went straight to voicemail. She knew he never answered calls when he was driving, so it didn't surprise her. She wasn't pleased when he hadn't arrived or called by the time they started lunch. One of the guests politely suggested that she hoped he hadn't had trouble on the road, or an accident, which hadn't occurred to Isabelle until then. She knew how much he disliked their party weekends, particularly when the guests were all her friends and none of his. Isabelle always thought their friends didn't mix well, so she invited her own. His "friends" were actually all business connections and Isabelle thought them bores, and their wives common.

By three-thirty, when they got up from the table after a delicious meal and more excellent wine, Isabelle looked mildly concerned, and said something to Stephanie when they were alone, after the guests dispersed to take walks or drive into the village.

"Do you suppose something happened to him? He's not answering his phone." It was four o'clock by then. "He's really pushing it this time. I know he hates these weekends with a house full of guests, but he can't just not show up at all. It looks terrible. Maybe something bad happened yesterday at the meeting and he's afraid to tell me." It seemed unlikely, but she lived in dread of his quitting in an angry moment, or getting fired during one of his heated arguments with Jerome. It was her worst fear after the two nightmarish years they had spent when he was unemployed, and she never wanted to lose the château.

"I'd probably be nervous by now too," Stephanie admitted. "Maybe you should call a few of the hospitals on the way, just so you know nothing happened to him. After that, you can be mad at him." Stephanie grinned and Isabelle laughed. "I'm sure he's fine, but you never know, and maybe he didn't want to worry you."

"That would be like him. He showed up once with a broken arm in a cast, after he fell down the stairs at his tennis club, and he never called to tell me. Mr. Macho, he never wants to admit it when he's hurt."

She went to her bedroom then, and called four hospitals between there and Paris, and none of them had a patient registered by that name. "So he's not hurt," she reported back to Stephanie before the guests returned from their wandering. "So can I get pissed now?" she asked her friend, and Stephanie laughed.

"Of course. You can raise holy hell when he shows up. This ought to be worth a very nice gift from Van Cleef, for standing up your guests and worrying you. You can tell him you cried all morning."

"You're an evil woman," Isabelle scolded her, but the plan sounded good to her too. Stephanie had a way of turning things to her advantage, and gave Isabelle good advice, as far as she was concerned. "I have to admit, I'm a little worried though. He's never been this late before."

"He's not stupid. He wouldn't go off with some tart as obviously as this. So at least you can be sure he's not with a woman. He's a lot smarter than that. He probably just didn't feel like showing up with all of us here. Or maybe he got sick, a nasty case of food poisoning." They went through various scenarios, and as the guests began to drift back, Isabelle put her concerns aside, and organized a bridge game, and some of them played poker. Her friends loved their weekends at the château. Isabelle knew how to throw a great house party. She played bridge with her guests and was an able player. She usually won, with Stephanie as her partner.

The small motorboat with two local fishermen in it stayed close to the shore, and they threw their lines in. Jacques and Emile had had a good day so far, and had caught enough fish for a good dinner and to sell some to the local market. It was a beautiful day, and the fish were plentiful. The two men had spent weekends fishing together for years. They didn't go out too far, and at one point had drifted closer to the shore than they intended, when one of them pulled something in on his line that was clearly not a fish. They couldn't tell what it was at first. It was a soggy black object that they landed in the boat, and saw that it was a wallet. One of them joked to the other that maybe there was money in it. They removed the hook that had caught on it, as water poured from it, and Jacques looked inside, and glanced up at his friend with wide eyes.

"We hit the lottery." The money was soaking wet, but undamaged. They pulled the money out and counted it. There were fourteen hundred euros in the wallet, a month's salary for either of them as a local carpenter and plumber. They saw then that there were credit cards too, and a soaking wet driver's license. The wallet belonged to a Charles Louis Vincent, with a Paris address on the license. Emile looked disappointed.

"It's too much money, we have to take it to the police. We can't keep it." Jacques agreed, and the credit cards forced their hands too. "He'll be happy to get his money back." They tossed the wallet onto a bench in the boat, and put bait on their hooks again. The wallet had been a good distraction for a minute, and they were going to take it to the police station at the end of the day. The owner might not even have reported it, if he knew he had dropped it in the sea and assumed it was gone forever, and it might have been if it weren't for two weekend fishermen. Fortunately for Charles Louis Vincent, whoever he was. A lucky devil to be sure. He hadn't lost his money or his credit cards, although he'd need a new wallet, and he'd have to replace his driver's license. They went on fishing for the rest of the afternoon, with the wallet drying in the sun, and the contents safe, found by two honest men. Lucky for him.

Aude slept for an hour, since she and Charlie hadn't slept much the night before. She lay in bed, breathing in Charlie's scent on the pillow, and then she finally got up, and went to wash their dishes. There were traces of him everywhere in her tiny cabin. She folded the blanket he had left on the couch when they went to her bedroom. She could still feel his gentle touch and remembered the look in his eyes. She had nothing left of him, except memories, and was looking forlorn as she put the blanket away in a cupboard, and gave a start when she heard a sound behind her. She turned and saw him standing there in the middle of her living room. Charlie looked serious as she gave a gasp and rushed toward him, he held her in his powerful arms, and she clung to him as he kissed her. She was breathless when they stopped and he was smiling at her.

"What are you doing here? I thought you'd be back at your house by now." She still didn't know it was a château, and wouldn't have cared.

"I changed my mind halfway there," he said, pulling her down on the couch next to him with an arm around her. "I thought about it for a minute, turned around, and came back here."

"Did you call?" He shook his head. "They must be worried sick about you."

"What if they're not? What if no one cares if I'm there or not?" He thought that a far more likely scenario, knowing Isabelle, and the people who were likely to be there that weekend. "They'll be drinking my wine and perfectly happy without me." He looked serious then. "I thought I'd steal a few days for us."

"How? Won't she call the police and look for you?"

"I didn't rob a bank, Aude. I fell off a cliff. I was thinking about saying I had an accident and hit my head, and was half conscious and confused for a few days. Something like that. My wife will be pissed more than scared. She probably doesn't really care if I show up or not. Just a few days, the weekend. I didn't want to leave you like that," he said, kissing her again.

"I didn't want you to go," she admitted, "but I knew you had to."

"Maybe I don't." He knew things like it happened all the time. People disappeared for a few days, and then surfaced with some unlikely excuse. Usually, in order to spend time with a girlfriend or a mistress or a boyfriend. All he knew was that he couldn't leave Aude just yet. He didn't know what they would do after this, but he had a powerful sense that something important had happened the night before. He wasn't ready for it to be over yet, and he wanted to steal all the time with her he could. He didn't care how angry Isabelle got. They hadn't slept together in years. He somehow felt it gave him the right to these stolen moments with the woman whose cabin he had walked into the night before, covered in blood and looking as though he'd been shipwrecked.

She was smiling broadly and loved the sound of his plan, although she felt slightly guilty for the worry they would cause his wife. But not guilty enough to tell him to leave. She didn't want to do that, and didn't have the strength to watch him drive away again. This felt like a gift from God, on top of his survival the night before. Maybe it was meant to be, for both of them.

"Maybe just a few days," she said, as he pulled her sweater over her head, and revealed her firm breasts. She hadn't worn a bra when they dressed that morning. Her body was exquisitely toned and firm, and he realized then that he didn't know how old she was. He knew nothing about her except that she was the most beautiful creature he'd ever seen, he'd never felt this way before, he was mad about her.

"How old are you?" he asked her.

"Why? Do you think I'm too old?" she asked him, worried, and he laughed.

"Too young maybe, but definitely not too old!

I'm fifty-three, and I want to know everything about you."

"I'm thirty-six," she said cautiously. He had guessed her to be thirty-two or -three when he thought about it on his way to the château.

"Where are you from? Where did you grow up?"

"In Bordeaux, until I went to the Beaux-Arts in Paris to study painting. I've lived here for eight years."

"Did you always paint?"

"Always, ever since I was a child."

"Do you have sisters or brothers?" She shook her head.

"I was an only child. My parents were older. They thought they couldn't have children, and I was a surprise. They were wonderful to me. They were both teachers."

"We have that in common. I'm an only child, and my mother was a professor at the Sorbonne. She was a great mother. My father was a fairly well-known writer. They died when I was young."

"Mine died in a fire in their home when I was at the Beaux-Arts. Their Christmas tree caught fire and they were trapped. They died on Christmas Eve. I sold their house and lived on that for a while, so I could continue to study painting. I sold my work at a gallery in Paris. They still sell work for me when I need the money." She smiled shyly.

"Do you have a boyfriend?" He looked concerned, and relieved when she shook her head.

"Have you ever been married?" She was slow to answer the question.

"I was," she said honestly. She didn't want to lie to him. "I got married in Paris after my parents died. I had no other family. My parents were only children too. I was lonely and scared. I met Paul through friends at the Beaux-Arts. He was a terrible person, but I was too young to realize it at first. He was very clever and lied a lot. He was insanely jealous, and beat me several times, just for talking to other men. Then I fell in love with a boy I had gone to school with in Bordeaux. He was at the Beaux-Arts too, studying architecture. He was kind and talented and a good person. My husband caught me with him one day. He beat me, and he killed him." She looked sorrowful when she said it. "He went to prison for it." Charlie frowned as he listened and held her hand. It was a terrible thing to happen to a young girl, alone in the world, with no family to protect her. She seemed so vulnerable, even now. Both fragile and strong at the same time.

"Where is he now?"

"Still in prison. I haven't heard from him in years. And I moved away so he could never find me when he got out. I divorced him when he went to prison. I cut off contact with everyone I knew in Paris, except my gallery, and started my life again here, where no one knew the story. I was ashamed. He won't be out for many years. He was sentenced to ten or twelve years. He's been in for eight. He was in the Réau prison last I knew."

"I'm sorry, Aude, that's an awful story. My history is a lot less exciting. I had good parents too. My father was strict and my mother loved to spoil me. I grew up in Paris, and was a pretty ordinary kid. My mother was a sweet woman, and my father was hard on me. He wanted me to be a writer, but I didn't have the talent, although I loved books, and reading, which is why I went into publishing. I went to HEC," the best business school in Paris, she knew, "went into publishing, got married young to a girl I knew as a student. She was smart and funny and I thought she was exciting. She was very bold and confident, which I admired. I think we started drifting apart when we had kids. She wanted a more glamorous life than I could give her, and that I was interested in. I didn't realize it then, we married so young, but she was spoiled and expected me to be someone I never wanted to be when we grew up. Things went along all right for about ten years. I worked in publishing and loved it.

"I had a hot temper when I was younger, had an argument with my bosses about the kind of books they wanted to publish. They wanted to get into soft porn and I thought it would cheapen the house. I walked out, and couldn't find another job for two years. Word got around in publishing that I was 'difficult,' and two years of being broke and out of a job killed our marriage. My wife made it very clear that she considered me a failure, which was hard for the kids too. They were young then, ten and sixteen. And we were very short of money for two years. By the time I found a job in another industry, our marriage was dead and she hated me. She never got over it and neither did I. I realized who she was then. It's been that way for thirteen years now, much too long to fix it. Neither of us wants to. It is what it is."

"That's a long time to be unhappily married," she said quietly.

"You get used to it. I don't expect it to change now. And I'm a man of principles and traditions, so I stayed."

"Did you cheat on her?" She wanted to know everything about him too.

"Yes." He was equally honest with her. "Just brief flings, and not very often. I never misled anybody. And I never fell in love again. I think that part of me died . . . until last night," he said softly, and he leaned over and kissed her. They had learned a lot about each other in a short time. They went back to her bedroom and made love again. But they weren't strangers anymore.

Afterwards, they went to the kitchen to get something to eat. There wasn't much in the fridge, and he looked at her in surprise. "Don't you eat?" She laughed at the question.

"Not much. The fridge is small, and I buy groceries every few days when I need them. I don't like cooking just for myself." He looked closely at her paintings then, and studied them carefully. She had talent and they were beautiful. She had a few still-lifes lined up against the wall, some haunting paintings of the ocean, and a portrait of a little girl with sad eyes who looked like her. "That's me as a child. I did it a few months ago."

"I thought it was."

"I tried to do one of my mother, but I could never get it right. Portraits are hard to do." She smiled at him then. "I'd love to do one of you." He was touched that she would say it.

"I think you should wait till my face heals." He smiled at her.

She made an omelet for them for lunch, and a salad, which they ate with bread and cheese, they shared a peach she had, and they each had a glass of wine, and then went back to bed and spent the rest of the afternoon there. She wanted to go to the farmer's market with him the next day. To Charlie, it was a perfect day, and exactly the life he wished he could live, in her small cozy cabin, making love to a woman he had fallen in love with. It was perfect and he couldn't think of a better life than this. It was the antithesis of the life he'd been living for so many years, with the grandeur of the château he had bought for Isabelle, their fancy Paris apartment, a job he never really cared about, and children he loved but didn't see enough of because they'd grown up. And, a woman who didn't love him, if she ever did. Being there with Aude was everything he had always dreamed of, and had told himself didn't exist, in order to continue living the empty life he had.

They drove to a beach nearby and walked in the sand, talking and laughing, and couldn't wait to get home to bed. They stopped at a bistro on the way back, in Vattetot-sur-Mer, and had a simple meal. He was embarrassed that he had to let her pay for it. He had no money now, and no credit cards.

"I'm keeping track, I'll pay you back when I have money. I already owe you for the rented car, and the clothes we bought this morning." It was hard to believe it had only been that morning when he tried to leave her and found he couldn't. And even stranger to believe he had only met her the night before. He had never been as comfortable with another human being, or known a woman he loved more. In twenty-four hours, his whole life had changed, when he went over a cliff into the ocean and didn't die. He had never felt more alive, as she paid for dinner, and they drove back to the cabin that felt like home to him now.

Chapter 4

On Saturday afternoon, someone driving through the area reported to the local police that there appeared to have been an accident. There was no sign of a vehicle, and no one visibly injured at the scene, but there were signs that a car had gone off the road and over the cliff, chunks of the edge of the road had fallen, and there were tire tracks leading down from there and on the shoulder. The driver reported it at the police station and drove on, and since there was no one injured, the police took their time checking it out. They had more important and pressing things to do. There had been a break-in in the next village, and a minor car accident an hour before, five miles up the road. A drunk had been found dead in a field. They had their hands full and it was late afternoon when they got to the scene of the supposed accident that they weren't sure of anyway. They studied the marks on the road when they got there, and the earth that had fallen away on the side of the road, where Charlie's car had gone down. They looked down the cliff face with binoculars, and saw small pieces of the car lodged between the rocks, bits of chrome, and the side mirror, shining in the sunlight, and the two policemen looked at each other after seeing the familiar signs.

"They were right, a car went down, but there's no sign of it." They agreed that the vehicle must have gone into the water. They would need divers to look for it, and the one or several bodies trapped inside. No missing persons had been reported in the last twenty-four hours, so it must have been someone passing through. It seemed odd that no one had reported it, but obviously there had been no observers of the accident, and there were no houses anywhere nearby.

The police called the Gendarmerie maritime for divers, but it was too late in the day for them to do anything about it. They promised to send a patrol boat with divers on Sunday morning. The tide had gone out, and the car could have traveled a good distance with the bodies in it. It was an ugly business, conducting a search like that. The police had no idea if anyone had been able to escape. The car could have gone down deep with people trapped inside and settled there. With luck, the divers would find whatever remained, both vehicular and human. They would have to deal with it the next day, even if they found any bodies washed up on a beach along the coastline. But there had been none reported so far.

The two fishermen with the wallet had stayed too long at the fish market selling their catch, and were going to turn in the wallet the next day too. It could wait. It wasn't going anywhere. It was safe with them. They were honest men.

At the château, Isabelle hosted another elegant dinner without Charlie and made excuses that were all lies, not to upset her guests. He'd never stayed out of touch for that long before. Only Stephanie knew that he was missing and that Isabelle was worried. "Do you suppose he's having an affair?" Isabelle asked her in a whisper after dinner. "What if he's had an accident and he's hurt and unconscious?"

"You called all the hospitals, and they didn't have anything," Stephanie reminded her. "Men are strange. Maybe he just needed a break. Martin did that to me once. He went to Monte Carlo and spent the weekend gambling, and showed up after three days. That's how I got my sapphire ring." She smiled at her. "Besides, the police would have called you if he'd had an accident. Your name must be on his papers as the person to call in an emergency. No, he's just having some kind of male meltdown, and is probably getting drunk somewhere. He'll probably show up tomorrow, and just didn't want to deal with weekend guests."

"He could at least call and tell me." Isabelle was half angry and half worried, alternately. "It's so damn inconsiderate of him." She and Charlie weren't in love, but they were married after all, and she cared about him.

"Men don't do things like that. They do what they want."

"You're right, he's obviously not hurt. He's just being a jerk." Isabelle reassured herself to justify being angry at him. Not showing up at all, he had embarrassed her with her guests.

"That would be my guess," Stephanie concluded about his being a jerk.

Isabelle went to bed mad at Charlie that night. He had never stayed away for a whole weekend before. She hoped he wasn't setting a new trend. Their marriage was already bad enough, without adding mysterious disappearances to it. She was tired of covering for him all weekend. She was going to give him hell when he finally turned up. She just hoped he hadn't quit his job or gotten fired or done something insane. She couldn't go through that again. Their life was just the way she wanted it now. And she had no intention of dealing with mysterious disappearances. She was going to leave him flat this time if he had quit his job. It took her a long time to fall asleep, thinking of how mad she was at him, and rehearsing what she would say when she saw him again, probably in the city on Sunday night. It seemed unlikely that he'd show up now at the château on Sunday, in time for the guests to leave. That would be unspeakably rude, if he arrived as they left.

The Gendarmerie maritime patrol boat with the divers showed up at nine o'clock on Sunday morning. They notified the local police in Vattetot when they began the search of the area, directly along the coastline. They saw no vehicle in the shallower water at first. But two hours later, they found it. It had traveled farther than they expected when the tide went out. The car was empty, and the driver's door was open. The vehicle had obviously been badly damaged when it fell. The seatbelt was unattached, so the driver either hadn't been wearing it or had freed himself, and with the door open on the driver's side, his body had obviously been swept out to sea and could turn up anywhere, or more likely not at all, and would either be attacked by fish, or pulled farther out to sea in deep water, where it would never be found. Clearly there were no survivors, and if there had been, the police would know by now. People didn't keep an accident like that a secret if they were alive.

The car would have to be brought to the surface by a salvage company. The divers made note of the license plate number, so the owner of the car could be researched, and the appropriate family members notified. The divers were back on board the patrol boat at noon in time for lunch. They were relieved not to have had to deal with bodies to bring to the surface. It was just a matter of bringing the car up now, which wasn't their job. They gave the police the license number, and their mission was accomplished.

The two fishermen turned in Charlie's wallet to the police station on their way back from church that morning. They handed it over, and the police logged it in, and there was no one to call, so they were going to wait for someone to claim it. They didn't connect it to the car the divers had found, a lost wallet in the ocean wasn't urgent, and with no survivors of the fallen car, they wouldn't have the registration information until Monday, when the department of vehicle registration opened. A young officer who came on duty that night raised the question, but it all had to wait until Monday morning now. They had had no missing person report, so no one was looking for the driver of the sunken vehicle. It was a mystery for the moment.

Isabelle's weekend guests left after lunch on Sunday, and thanked her profusely for a wonderful weekend. She drove back to the city alone that afternoon in a fury. Stephanie went back to Paris with Edmond. Isabelle fully expected to see Charlie in the apartment, with some lame excuse about why he hadn't shown up, and she was planning to raise hell with him for standing her up, along with all their weekend guests, and leaving her to deal with them alone. She didn't mind dinners alone, but an entire weekend with no call from him and having to make excuses for him was just too much.

She was startled when she saw no one in the darkened apartment, and no note from Charlie. Whatever he was doing, he still hadn't come home, and at first she was even madder, but by late Sunday night she was genuinely worried and called Stephanie.

"He still hasn't come home. I think something is wrong. I'm going to call the police tomorrow and report him as missing."

"If something bad had happened, the police would have called you," Stephanie said, still assuming the worst of Charlie, and some form of misbehavior. She wasn't worried, which calmed Isabelle somewhat. Stephanie was right, the police would have called her if something was seriously wrong, like an accident on the road. Isabelle had driven past the place where he had gone over the cliff on the way home, and never noticed. She was on the other side of the road, looking straight ahead as she drove. She slept fitfully that night and was planning to call the police on Monday morning, after she called Charlie's office to see if he had shown up there. Anything was possible at this point.

Aude and Charlie went to the farmer's market in Vattetot on Sunday, and bought groceries. They cooked dinner together on Sunday night, and Aude looked at him seriously after the meal.

"When are you planning to go back?" She wanted some warning, so she could prepare herself for it. They had spent forty-eight magical hours together, and neither of them wanted it to end, but she knew it had to at some point. He had a life to go back to, a job, a wife, and a family.

"I've been thinking about it," he said just as seriously. He had said when he came back on Saturday morning that he wanted a few days with her before he left. He hadn't had enough of her yet, and he wanted more. "Maybe in a few days."

"Can you do that? What about work?"

"They can live without me for a few days."

"And what about your wife? Isn't it cruel to leave her with no news at all? She must be worried sick by now. I would be."

"That's you, not her. I'm sure she had a great weekend with her friends. By now, she's probably ready to kill me, but I'm sure it's not breaking her heart to have me disappear for a weekend. I don't want to go back, Aude. People do things like this every day, disappear for a while, some people do it forever." He had been thinking of that too, but didn't want to scare her if he told her. "Some people get an opportunity like this and never go back."

"Would you do something like that?" She looked shocked. "That doesn't seem like you." She could tell he was a responsible person, not just someone who would walk out on his life, but it was clear to her how unhappy he was at home and in his work. "What about your kids?" He talked about them a lot with love and pride. She couldn't imagine his abandoning them.

"That would be the hard part. I'd contact them eventually. I couldn't live with never seeing my kids again. I just want time with you, that's all. I can't go back yet. I don't want to." She saw his jaw set in a hard line when he said it, which she hadn't seen before. That was new. It was all new between them right now. They had much to learn about each other. "I don't know if I will go back. Maybe this is my one chance to free myself, and build a new life."

"You can't do that if it means hurting people. That's not who you are." She already knew that much about him.

"I'm not sure who I am right now. I've been given a ticket to freedom. I want to run with it before someone takes it away and locks me up in my cage again. The life I've been leading means nothing to me. There's nothing I want in that life. Everything I want now is here."

"How would you live?" He smiled at the question.

"I can get a job. I could work at your car mechanic's garage. I used to be good with cars when I was a kid." They had returned the car he had rented. He didn't need it now. He wasn't going anywhere.

"Is that what you want? To be a car mechanic now?" She was surprised by what she was hearing. It seemed unlike him from all she had learned in a few days, about his education, his jobs, his responsibilities.

He laughed at her question. "Maybe. It might be fun for a while."

"Charlie, be serious. I want you to stay too. But it's a big deal walking out on a life like yours, and letting your family think you're dead."

"They'll have everything they need. I'm sure Isabelle would prefer it. My kids would be sad, for a while, but I hardly see them now. I could contact them eventually. I just don't want to go back to Isabelle and my job. I want to stay here with you." He felt irresponsible for the first time in his life and was actually enjoying it. He felt free.

"There are other ways to do that," she said sensibly.

"I know. And maybe that's what I'll do eventually. Right now, I want to disappear, just slip away in the night and have a life with you, right here, right now. We're already here, doing it. I'm not going back for now. Is it okay with you if I stay here?" She nodded. "I'll leave if you want me to."

"I don't want you to leave, but I don't want you to create a mess for yourself either."

"I can always say I had amnesia. People do that too."

"People do a lot of things. You're really going to let them think you're dead?"

"I think I am, for a while. I was dead before. I'm alive now. More alive than I've been in my entire life, because of you. I can get up in the morning and do what I want."

"Then go back and quit your job, and leave Isabelle. In the long run, I think you have to be honest with them, all of them. That's who you are."

"It's who I've always been. Right now, I want to be dead for a while. It's so much simpler. I've already disappeared. I just have to keep going on the path I'm on." She could see that he meant it and that it was what he wanted to do. She wondered how long it would last, and how long he would want a simple life, with her, and a local job.

"I want a different life from the one I had. I haven't figured out how to do that yet, and until I do, I'm just going to disappear. And if you ever want me to go, just tell me, and I'll leave," he said. He didn't want to impose on her.

"I don't want you to leave, I want you to stay,"

she said in a soft, husky voice. "I've been waiting for you all my life. I don't want to lose you. I just don't want you to do something you'll regret later."

"I have no regrets about what I'm doing. I'm sure of it. I've never been so sure about anything in my life." She smiled and he put his arms around her and held her. For a dead man, he was the happiest he'd ever been in his life.

On Monday morning, the police in Vattetot-sur-Mer checked the license number on Charlie's car, and got the information that it was registered to Charles Louis Vincent in Paris. There was an office number to call and a home number and address. The same young officer checked the ID in the wallet the fishermen had turned in. It was a match, and it instantly became a whole different story. Charles Vincent had obviously gone over the cliff, was in the car when it plunged into the water, had lost his wallet in the process, and had been swept out to sea. His body hadn't turned up and probably never would. But it was obvious that he had died under the water somewhere in the area, and his body had gone out with the tide, and vanished into the depths of the ocean. The police officer doubted he would ever be found. Or if he were, his remains might turn up far down the coast, but it was unlikely.

And now they had to call the next of kin, his

wife, and notify her of her husband's death. They called the police department of the 7th Arrondissement where the couple lived. The police station promised to send officers to Isabelle's apartment to see her within the hour. The local police in Normandy didn't envy them the task. It surprised them that no one had reported him missing, but maybe his family hadn't figured it out yet, or didn't even know he was gone.

The police car parked in front of the building on the Champ de Mars at two in the afternoon, and two police officers got out. After the manager of the building let them in the outer door, they buzzed the intercom, and Isabelle answered. She saw on the video screen that they were police officers, and buzzed them in. She had a terrible feeling when she did, that something bad was about to happen. She led them into her living room when they got to the apartment, and she invited them to sit down, while she waited for them to tell her what she didn't want to hear.

They explained the accident to her, what they could guess about it, what must have happened to the car, how it had disappeared under the water and been pushed far by the currents. They explained how her husband's body had floated free of it and must have been swept toward the open ocean. They told her that it was unlikely they would ever find the body, but that there was no doubt that her husband had died, drowned in the car, either during or after the accident. They were very sorry, and stayed with her until she regained her composure. She was in shock. Charlie was dead. He had vanished on Friday night, as closely as they could figure it. The more senior of the two officers explained to her that the police would provide a statement that would confirm her husband's death in circumstances they felt certain of, with the evidence at hand. Without a body, she would have to have the police statement confirmed in court. She would then receive a death certificate, which would allow his life insurance to be paid, his will to be acted on, his estate and any other bequests to be distributed to his heirs. The officers assured Isabelle that in this case there was no question in their minds that Charles Vincent was dead, that he could not have survived the accident, or his car going down in the ocean. The court hearing would only be a formality, so that the will could be executed.

Isabelle had no idea what arrangements Charlie had made or if there were any that involved her. She could easily imagine her life crumbling around her, and even losing the château, if Charlie hadn't provided for it, and the upkeep. She didn't know if he had life insurance, or if she could afford the death taxes. She suddenly realized how much she didn't know. He hadn't planned to die. She hadn't even cried yet. She was too shocked. She called Stephanie as soon as the police had left.

"He's dead," were her first words over the phone.

"Who's dead?" Stephanie didn't understand.

"Charlie. He went over a cliff in an accident, and drowned, on his way to the château. He was dead all weekend while we had the house party." Isabelle felt sick while she thought of it. And she'd kept wondering when he'd show up.

"Oh my god. No. That's not possible. Why didn't the police call you?"

"They didn't have the information about the car registration until this morning. The car was on the ocean floor, and still is. They just left. I have to call his boss. Steph, I have no idea how to do this. And what if he didn't leave enough money, or leave it to me? I could lose everything." She was already thinking of her future, minutes after she had learned of his death. More important than the château or the money, she had lost him, but the château was what came to mind first. "His body was swept out to sea. I have to go to court to get the death certificate, based on the police report."

"He was a responsible guy. He wouldn't leave you stranded," Stephanie said quietly, shocked too.

"It's happened to other people. It could happen to me."

"I'll be there in ten minutes. Just sit tight, we'll

figure it out. And you have to tell the kids, before they hear it from someone else."

"No one knows yet except you." Isabelle felt like she was in a haze. She was too terrified to cry. All she could think of now was Charlie, what he had left her, and how she would survive. As she thought of him going over the cliff, hitting the rocks below and disappearing into the ocean forever, she couldn't even imagine it, and didn't want to. She hoped he hadn't suffered. And now she had to tell their children. She had no idea how she was going to get through the days ahead. She wanted to be angry at him, but she wasn't, or even sad. All she felt now was scared, for herself.

Chapter 5

Isabelle felt like a robot when she opened the door to Stephanie. She arrived twenty minutes after Isabelle's call, and she looked just as shocked as the widow. It was hard to think of Isabelle that way as they walked into the living room together and sat down. They were sitting exactly where the police had. Isabelle was still trying to understand what they'd said. She told Stephanie the details again. It made no more sense and was no easier to believe in the second telling than in the first.

"He left the city late," Isabelle said softly. "The police think he must have fallen asleep at the wheel, or somehow lost control of the car. He may not even have woken up until he hit the rocks and the water, but he couldn't have stopped the fall once he was over the edge anyway. He was doomed from then on." Isabelle noticed that Stephanie was looking at her strangely, as though she didn't believe what Isabelle had said.

"What?" she said nervously. "I'm telling you what the police told me. It's all guesswork, except for the fact that his car went over the edge. They could see his tire tracks clearly in the dirt, and they found the car fifteen feet down in the water. It's not hard to figure out," she snapped at her, stressed by everything that had happened. "They said he was certainly dead."

"I just had a strange thought," Stephanie said. "Sometimes people fake their own death and use an opportunity like this to step out of their lives and just walk away, and start a new life somewhere else. I'm not saying he did. But it's kind of a weird thought. Or maybe he was depressed and did it on purpose."

"The police asked me that too, if I thought it was possible he was suicidal, if he was in financial trouble of some kind."

"And what did you tell them?"

"That there's no way he would have committed suicide. He loved me and the kids too much to run out on us or kill himself." She was definite about it, as though trying to convince herself.

"Maybe take a brief leave of absence?" Stephanie pressed her.

"Not even that. That's a disgusting idea. Charlie would never shirk his responsibilities. He would never run away, not even for a few days. He wasn't that kind of man. I told them that myself."

"So what do you think really happened?" Stephanie asked her bluntly. "What does your gut say?"

"My gut and my brain are on pause," Isabelle said, "but I think it happened the way they said. He fell asleep at the wheel, and went off the edge of a cliff. I don't think he was depressed. He didn't suffer from depression. He had no reason to commit suicide, or to fake his death and disappear. He was a happy man with a perfect life. He loved the kids and me. We may not have been madly in love anymore, but we had a great life, and he had a terrific job. He had everything he wanted." She sounded certain of it, and Stephanie looked at her intensely, not as sure.

"Did he? You two haven't been happy together in a long time, and a job in plastics was never his dream. He loved his old job, he always said so, and he blew that with a temper tantrum. He hated his current boss even more than the last one, and you said yourself, Charlie was always having arguments with him. Maybe that's what happened on Friday night and it was why he was late. Maybe it was one fight too many in a job he hated. Who wouldn't want to walk out on their life sometimes? It's the perfect fantasy. Something happens and you just get up and leave and disappear, and get rid of all the problems in one fell swoop. I could see Charlie doing that. He wasn't a fighter. I think he'd sooner just disappear than fight for freedom and respect."

"I respected him," Isabelle said, looking offended. She didn't know what her friend was saying or why. Stephanie could be harsh at times, but she always called things as she saw them, and she didn't mince words with Isabelle. Stephanie wasn't a kind woman, but she was always a straight shooter and spoke her mind, especially with her closest friend.

"*Did* you respect him?" Stephanie said pointedly, and Isabelle looked uncomfortable. "I wonder if he thought so."

"Of course he did. He had a bad run of luck thirteen years ago. He got over it and wound up with a better job."

"Better for who? You got everything you wanted out of it when he got the job at Jansen. What did he get? A big title and a big salary. Your marriage never recovered from it. You've said so yourself. Look, I don't know what happened, and you knew him better than I did, you're his wife. I'm just saying people do weird things sometimes. If he could have gotten out of the car once it hit the water, he had an opportunity. I don't know if he took it or not, but sometimes people do strange things. Did he have any heavy debts?" Stephanie didn't know why, but she was suspicious of their not finding the body, despite the police officers' explanation for it, which was logical but not entirely convincing. Isabelle didn't question it. She believed the police and was annoyed at Stephanie for questioning what they said, and having theories of her own that were unsettling. Sometimes Stephanie liked to make trouble just for the hell of it.

"No, he didn't have debts," Isabelle responded. "He wasn't a gambler."

"Sometimes it's the straight-up responsible guys that surprise you. I guess you're right though. Charlie wasn't the kind of man who'd walk out on you. He wouldn't have wanted to let you or anyone else down. He didn't like disappointing people. It just seemed like an interesting idea."

"This isn't a novel, or a TV series," Isabelle said, annoyed at her friend. "It's real life. No one sane just gets up and walks out on a family, a career, a whole life." People did, but Stephanie agreed with her, not many. In an odd way it seemed like an act of courage to do so, not a cowardly act, which some people might not believe. "He'd never do that to the kids," Isabelle said firmly.

"So what happens now?" Stephanie asked her.

"I have to plan a funeral . . . and I have to tell Jerome Jansen and the children what happened. I keep thinking Charlie is going to walk into the room and tell me it was all a mistake, and his car broke down somewhere."

"I have the same feeling," Stephanie admitted. "It doesn't seem real yet. One minute he's here and then he's not. And a funeral without a body always seems odd."

"He might still wash up on a beach somewhere, but the police didn't think so. If he was pulled out far enough by the tides, they'll never find him. So I'll have to get the death certificate in court, based on the conclusive police report."

Isabelle called Jerome Jansen after that, and there was silence on the line after she told him.

"It happened on Friday night?" he asked her, sounding shaken.

"They think so. No one saw it happen. Some fishermen found his wallet on Saturday morning, so it happened before that. He was supposed to come to the château for dinner. We had weekend guests. He was waiting to meet with you, and he must have left later than he said he would."

"We had a disagreement about some warning stickers," Jerome said, feeling guilty now. "We didn't need to put them on, and he was afraid some kid would get hurt on our new trampolines. He was always overly cautious. Are the police sure he died when the car went down?"

"They said there's no way he could have survived it. It's a huge drop from where he went off the road, and the car went straight down to the rocks below, into the water, and sank." They were both quiet for an instant, imagining it. It seemed like a horrible way to die. She hoped it had been quick. And drowning sounded awful too.

"I'm sorry, Isabelle. Is there anything I can do to help?" Jerome offered.

"Did he have a pension?" she asked him bluntly.

"Of course, but not for life. At his age, I think he was covered for a year or two, and we never talked about it, but I'm sure he had insurance. He would have wanted to provide for you if something happened." Jerome knew she was an expensive woman with high expectations of her husband. Charlie had alluded to it occasionally. He had spent a fortune on the château to keep her happy and restore their marriage. Jerome wasn't sure it had. Charlie had never seemed happily married to him. He was resigned. Jerome was never sure why Charlie had worked so hard to please Isabelle. It never seemed like a love match to him, but Charlie was that kind of guy, who'd go the extra mile for his wife and family. "Do you know when the funeral will be?"

"I haven't even started making the arrangements. I called you first. I haven't even told the kids yet."

"Thank you for letting me know. I'm going to miss him terribly. He fought with me like a devil, but it was always in the spirit of what was best for the business. He had our best interests at heart, even when I didn't agree with him." It was a generous statement, coming from Jerome. Isabelle had never liked him. She thought he was common and had bad manners, and she knew Charlie thought so too. But the high salary Jerry paid him made up for a lot, in her mind anyway. "I'll see you at the funeral."

They hung up and Stephanie handed her a glass of wine, before she called the kids. It was as hard as she'd expected. Judith was devastated. It was early in New York, and she hadn't left for work yet. She told her mother she'd take a flight as soon as she could get one. She had idolized her father, and was a lot like him. Principled, honest, responsible, reliable, with a kind heart. Olivier was just as shocked, and worried about his mother. He said he'd take the Eurostar immediately and be home in a few hours. He cried when she told him, and Judith had sobbed and could barely speak during the call. She couldn't imagine her life without her father to talk to and his sound, sensible advice on every subject. Charlie spoke with Judith more often than he did with Olivier, who was older and more independent, and didn't see either of them often now that they were grown up and working abroad. They spoke to their mother even less often. Charlie was warmer and more approachable. He never wanted to be strict and rigid like his own father, and had always been warm and open with his children, more so than Isabelle. She had felt that her job as a mother was over when they turned eighteen and left for college. Charlie never agreed and considered fatherhood a lifetime commitment. Once the children left, Isabelle was always busy with her friends and some project at the château, like her gardens, or a party she was planning which superseded everything else. Charlie always made time for them, no matter how busy he was. Now the voice of reason would be gone, and so would the father who loved them. They never said it but they both knew that their mother was self-centered more than maternal.

Thinking about it pained Charlie too, and leaving his kids was almost enough to make him give up his fantasy and go home. He just wanted a little more time with Aude before he did. He wasn't planning to abandon them forever. But for once, he wanted to think of himself. He had never done that in his entire life.

It wouldn't have surprised Charlie to know that as soon as Jerome hung up after speaking to Isabelle, he called the production department and canceled the warning stickers he and Charlie had argued about. He felt better after he did. But he was going to miss Charlie anyway. He was a smart, decent, hardworking guy. Jerome suspected the waters would close over him at home quickly. Isabelle wasn't a woman to waste time. Jerome was sure she'd marry again if she could find a willing man rich enough, or maybe Charlie had left her well-off enough so she wouldn't have to. But she struck him as the kind of woman who wouldn't mourn her husband for long. She had her château to show off with, and he could imagine her giving the grand parties Charlie had hated and complained about. There was nothing to stop her now. She had spent his money liberally when he was alive, and Jerome could see her doing it even more so as a widow. It was strange to think that Charlie was gone. But that was how it happened. One day you had a life, and then in a single instant, with no warning in most cases, it was over, and whatever you had tried to achieve in your lifetime and thought was so important no longer mattered. Life was like that. At eighty-two, Jerome often thought of it. He had his son in LA whom he only saw once or twice a year, and barely knew now. They had become strangers to each other years before. An accident like Charlie's made you wonder what it was all about, and whether or not it was worth it. It was odd how the good guys died, and sometimes the bad ones lived forever, or seemed to. He had seen enough of life at his age to know that was true. Too often the good died young.

He was feeling sentimental about it as he wiped a tear from his cheek and walked out of his office, after he canceled the stickers. He was happy about getting his way on that at least, without another battle. Charlie had been a noble fighter for all the causes he believed in. Jerome respected him for that, and knew he'd miss him. He'd been closer to Charlie than to his own son. Now he'd have to look for another CEO. He knew he was lucky to have had Charlie running the company for eleven years. He had done a good job and had made improvements that would outlive him now. He had forged their greatest success and multiplied the value of the company exponentially, to everyone's benefit.

After Isabelle had told the children, she called the funeral home and the church. She explained that there wouldn't be a body or a casket. She didn't see any point having a symbolic empty casket and preferred to make it a memorial service. It was late afternoon by the time she had finished making the arrangements. She sat in her study, staring into space. Stephanie had gone home, and Olivier was due home from London any minute. Judith was arriving from New York later that night. Everything had a feeling of unreality to it. Isabelle walked into Charlie's dressing room on the way to her bathroom, and stood staring at his clothes. Everything looked as though he would be home any minute, and it was impossible to believe he was gone. It just didn't seem possible. She was still so shocked she felt numb.

She hadn't had time to speak to Charlie's lawyer, Philippe Delacroix. She had been too busy making arrangements for the funeral. She still had to speak to the florist in the morning, and pick the music for the service. The funeral home was going to take care of the programs, and she had to pick a photo for them, and talk to her caterer about a reception at the house after the memorial service.

She wanted to speak to the lawyer most of all. She was eager to know what was in Charlie's will, how well he had provided for her, and if the château was safe. With Charlie gone, she had to think of herself. She had gotten through the whole day without crying, but as she thought about how unprotected she was now, with Charlie no longer there to take care of her, she lay down on her bed and sobbed, not for the man she had lost, but the lifestyle she feared he might have taken with him. If she lost that too, she would miss it most of all.

While Isabelle was frantically making funeral arrangements in the city, Charlie and Aude drove to the village in her beaten-up old car. She didn't care how it looked. It was functional and got her where she needed to go. That was good enough for her. Appearances had never mattered to her, and still didn't. She lived frugally and very carefully on what she made from her art. Charlie teased her when he saw the age and condition of her car.

He wanted to get them both cell phones. He thought particularly Aude should have a new one. He bought his under a fictitious name and used her address. They gave him a very low limit, but he didn't mind. He wasn't planning to make calls, except to her, if they went somewhere separately. He wanted to pay for both phones, and told her to put it on the growing list of things he planned to repay her for, once he had some cash in hand. And there was only one way he was going to achieve that, get a job.

He walked into the garage while Aude went to the post office. She was sending some sketches to her gallery in Paris. He was smiling and looked relaxed when he met her at her car twenty minutes later.

"What have you been up to?" she asked him casually.

"I just got a job. Armand hired me three days a week. He might give me a fourth, if he likes my work," he said proudly.

"Just like that? You're now a car mechanic?" She looked amused.

"Just like that. You can't support me forever, and I know a lot about cars, especially old ones," he said, and leaned over and kissed her. She had never been with a man who cared about supporting her before. The previous men in her life hadn't hesitated to take advantage of her, no matter how little she had. Charlie was an entirely different kind of man, and he knew she needed the money she was spending on him so generously. "I start tomorrow. I'll give you my first few paychecks. That should do it, except he wants to pay me cash," which was better for Charlie anyway. He wanted there to be no trace that could lead to his whereabouts, or let anyone know that he was alive. Aude had already volunteered to do his banking for him, but he didn't want to cause her any more trouble than he already had. She had been a good sport about it, but he didn't like owing her money she needed for herself.

They went back to her place to cook dinner. He would have liked to have dinner with her in the bistro in the village, but until the scrapes on his face healed, that didn't seem prudent, in case people put two and two together and guessed who he was. Or wondered how his face had gotten so battered.

They spent a quiet evening that night, while he tried not to guess what was happening in Paris. He had heard at the garage that the car had been found and identified, so he assumed that plans for his funeral were under way by then, and that the children would be arriving after their mother had told them that he'd been in a fatal accident. He cringed, imagining how his children had reacted, and how distraught Judith must have been. He had always been her protector and now he wasn't there, which made him feel guilty. He hated to be the one who caused them pain. It didn't change his resolve to step out of his old life and start a new one. There were a lot of things and emotions happening at once. Beginning a new life, and letting go of the old one.

He could imagine Isabelle calling Jerome, and his more candid response. He was sure too that as soon as she contacted him, Jerome had canceled the warning stickers Charlie had fought so hard for.

It seemed ghoulish but Charlie was curious

about what kind of funeral Isabelle would arrange for him. He suspected it would be pompous, showy, and traditional, which would impress the people who mattered to her, not something that would be meaningful, warm, or representative of him. He would have preferred something simple, more like the life he was leading now, and had just fallen into. Literally by accident, he had found a path he wanted to follow, not the one he had pursued for years, according to what Isabelle wanted or thought was suitable, with little or no regard for who he was, or his needs.

He wondered now if Isabelle knew him at all, or had ever wanted to. Their life had been all about her, and the path she expected him to follow, and he had always adjusted to her. His greatest regret now was how willing he had been to give up his own needs in favor of hers. He wondered why he had believed hers more important than his own. The simple world he had fallen into with Aude suited him so much better than the victories he had thought so valid and even crucial before. He felt as though he had been released from prison, and it was hard to imagine going back now, or wanting to.

Charlie slept peacefully that night, lying next to Aude. He got up early the next morning, dressed in jeans and a shirt she'd bought him, and was drinking coffee and making toast when Aude wandered into the kitchen, half asleep. She looked beautiful

with her disheveled long blond hair and her innocent face. She was wearing one of her old shirts,
her long legs naked and enticing.

"You're up early. And you're all dressed," she
said as she sat down and he handed her the strong
coffee she liked to drink, as though they'd been
doing it for years.

"I'm going to work." He smiled at her.

"At the garage? You're serious about it?" She
was still amazed. Charlie was a man of many facets
and some surprises, more so than she'd expected.

"Of course. Armand needs help. I used to be
pretty good at rebuilding engines and working on
old cars." She admired him for trying to build a
new life and working at a job so far beneath what
he was capable of. He looked happy about it. "It's
going to be fun."

"Take my car to get to work." She had already
told him he could, and he thanked her, bent to kiss
her, and left a few minutes later. She listened to her
old car rattle down the dirt road next to her house
and disappear.

She studied her latest painting, and got to work
on it a little while later. She'd had an idea for something she wanted to add on it, and was happy to
have a day to work, without the temptation of
wanting to spend all her time with him in bed.
They were trying to find where "normal" was in the
new life they were building together. He acted as
though he intended to stay, which she still found

hard to believe. She was afraid that one day she'd wake up, and he would have gone back to his old life. She couldn't imagine him existing in hers forever, or even for very long. Everything in it was foreign to him, except her. He felt as though he'd known her all his life, and she felt the same about him. The days and nights they were sharing were magical.

He thought about her on the way to work. She would be exciting to come home to, after a day of earnest manual labor. He had always liked projects where he could see what he had accomplished by the end of the day. He didn't have to wait a year to see a prototype, or for it to be tested, approved, and take another two years to produce. Manual work was going to be immediate in its satisfaction and rewards.

Armand was waiting for him at the garage, happy to see him. He was looking forward to having company while he worked, and not having to shoulder the weight of everything alone. He had four daughters and had never managed to have a son he could bring into his business. It was lucky for him that Aude's new friend was looking for a job. He didn't know how long he'd stay, but he was grateful for whatever time he could get, and Charlie seemed like a bright guy, and said he knew cars and could do the work. Armand was curious to see if he was all talk, or knew what he was doing. A lot of guys said they knew engines, and it was nothing more than a hobby to them. Armand explained carefully what he wanted him to do, and Charlie put on a pair of overalls, picked up a box of tools, and got to work, sliding under an old truck.

Armand came to check on him several times, and by lunchtime, he was impressed. Charlie knew what he was doing, didn't talk a lot, and had located an additional problem Armand had missed himself.

"Good work," he said as he watched him, and they went across the street to the coffee shop for lunch. Most days, Armand brought lunch from home, but he hadn't today. They each paid their part, and were back at work an hour later. Charlie didn't waste time. It was almost the end of the day when a flatbed truck pulled up, with the wreckage of a car secured to it. The men who'd brought the truck asked where to put the wreck, and Armand directed them where to unload it behind the garage. Charlie recognized it immediately. It was the remains of his car.

"There's nothing for you to salvage on this one. The police told us to bring it here," they told Armand as Charlie watched, realizing again how lucky he was to be alive.

"There can't have been any survivors in this one," Armand said, as Charlie stood silently by, and didn't volunteer any information, or admit he owned the car. "It happened over the weekend. Whoever was in it washed out to sea. The Gendar-

merie maritime divers found it five meters down."
Armand commented that he'd seen worse wrecks
before, but not many. They went back to work then,
and he remarked to Charlie that they'd have to get
it to the scrapyard fifty miles away, and borrow a
truck to do it.

At the end of the day, Armand thanked him for
a good day's work, and Charlie said he'd see him
tomorrow. He stopped to buy a paper on the way
home, and opened it to the obituary page. He saw
his immediately, with a ten-year-old photo of him
in a business suit and tie. He remembered when it
was taken, about a year after he'd gone to work for
Jerome, and had gone to a conference with him in
New York. It was a photo of a serious-looking businessman. In a matter of days, he couldn't remember being that person anymore. He was looking at
a stranger's face, not even someone he'd want to
know, let alone be. It was a relic of another life. He
took the paper with him, to read it carefully when
he got home to Aude.

When he walked into the house, he found her in
the kitchen, concentrating on the painting she had
worked on since that morning, and she seemed satisfied with the result. She broke into a broad smile
as soon as she saw him.

"How was work?" She sounded like a mother
asking him about school.

"I loved it." He looked as happy as she did. He
didn't tell her that they'd brought his car into the

garage. He dropped the paper on the kitchen table, and she put her arms around him and kissed him. "Maybe I should have stayed home with you today," he said in a husky voice, nuzzling her neck. He forgot all about the obituary he wanted to read, until after he'd made love to her, and they were figuring out what to make for dinner. He noticed then that there was an article about him on the front page too, a news item that a respected CEO had died in an accident on the Normandy coast on Sunday. It gave the pertinent details of his career.

He read both the article and the obituary, while Aude got dinner started. They were having blood sausage, fresh string beans from the farmer's market, and Brie with a fresh baguette. He handed her the paper, and she read down the litany of his accomplishments.

"Very impressive," she said quietly. "Are you happy with it?"

"Not really," he admitted. She had thought that from the look on his face. "None of that stuff matters. It seems so insignificant. That's all that's left of thirty years. None of it says who I really was, what kind of human being. I could have been beating my wife or abusing my children, and I could still have accomplished the same things. There's no humanity to it, nothing personal or real. It sounds like a wasted life to me, nothing to be proud of."

"You made the front page though." She smiled at him, and he shrugged with a wry grin.

"I guess I did. And all I had to do was fall thirty feet down a cliff and wind up in the ocean to do it . . . and find you." He smiled at her and kissed her. "Now that would have been newsworthy. The rest . . . it's just like reading a CV . . . it's all been done before, and you don't need to be a great human being to do it." It made Charlie more certain than ever that he had done the right thing when he decided not to go back. It had been the best decision he'd ever made, and the only one he didn't regret now. Reading the summary of his life in the paper made it that much easier to walk away.

Chapter 6

Charlie's funeral at the Basilica of Sainte-Clotilde was what everyone would have expected. The church itself, in the fashionable 7th Arrondissement, was where many social and wealthy people attended church on Sunday, got married, had their children baptized, and were buried. Isabelle knew one of the priests there. It was Isabelle and Charlie's parish, so the priests readily accepted her holding the funeral for Charlie there, although they had never attended church regularly.

Isabelle's father was shocked and saddened by the sudden loss of a respectful son-in-law who had fulfilled his obligations to his father-in-law's satisfaction. Charlie hadn't turned out to be the fiery success he had hoped for his daughter, but he had adequately redeemed himself with his lucrative job at Jansen Plastics and provided well for her. And

Isabelle's father was sorry for her to be widowed so young. But at fifty-two, having taken good care of herself and with Charlie's assets and the château, he was sure she would attract a suitable second husband soon, perhaps even a better one, a man with greater influence and means, who had sought to make a more impressive mark on the world than Charlie had achieved. Charlie's father-in-law had set the bar high for him.

At the funeral, Isabelle played the role of grieving widow well, in a black Chanel suit she and Stephanie had picked together, with a chic black hat Stephanie loaned her. Judith wore a simple black dress borrowed from her mother, and Olivier a black suit he had left at his parents' apartment, because he never wore it. The immediate family looked somber and subdued in the front pew at Ste-Clotilde, with three hundred mourners behind them, and everyone looking shocked and serious at the startling circumstances that had ended Charlie's life at fifty-three.

Judith had her father's dark hair and eyes and her mother's slim figure. She was a beautiful girl, and would be more so as she matured. She still looked like a schoolgirl in the serious black dress that was a little too big for her. She cried through the entire service, holding tightly to her brother's hand. Stephanie was in the front pew with them, on Isabelle's other side, and Olivier tried to look worthy of his new role as the head of the family now at twenty-nine. He had taken three days off from his job in London to be with his mother and sister, and he would have been a pallbearer had there been a casket. His grandparents and his aunts and uncles filled the pew behind Isabelle and her children. Olivier and Judith scarcely knew their mother's relatives since neither she nor Charlie ever thought them of interest. Charlie liked some of them but never made the effort to maintain contact with them. He was too busy.

Everything about the service was proper and appropriate. The priest's eulogy spoke of Charlie's successful career and the family he had left behind, his loving wife, his lovely daughter, and a son who was following in his father's footsteps, making his father so proud. There was nothing to suggest that he would be greatly missed, except the devastated look on his daughter's face. Isabelle sat erect and dignified for the duration of the mass, and it was impossible to see her face behind the short veil on the elegant hat. She looked beautiful, composed, and chic, which wouldn't have surprised Charlie. He would have expected nothing less of her, and he would have been even less surprised by the lack of warmth of the service, which reflected how Isabelle had organized it. The flowers were exquisite, by one of the best florists in Paris. The large arrangements of white flowers would have been equally appropriate for a wedding. Nothing about it seemed personal, nor was anything reminiscent of Charlie.

It was the funeral of a successful businessman who in the end had left little mark on the world, and had made no great difference, except to the handful of people who knew him well.

Jerome Jansen sat in the pew behind Isabelle's parents and sisters, and their spouses. They all sat quietly through the mass. And in the pews behind them, Isabelle's friends and a few of Charlie's, mainly from publishing where he had been well liked and appreciated and missed when he left. There was nothing remarkable about Charlie's funeral. Afterwards, almost everyone went to their apartment for an equally elegant reception, lavishly orchestrated by Isabelle like everything else. No friends of Charlie's had spoken at the funeral. Isabelle didn't want people speaking because she couldn't predict or control what would be said. Judith was too distraught to do a Bible reading, and Olivier preferred not to if his sister didn't, and it wasn't appropriate for Isabelle to do so as the widow.

Everything went smoothly, and when the last guest left, Judith was asleep in her room, Olivier had gone out to be with his friends, and Isabelle collapsed in a chair, with Stephanie looking alert and ready to gossip about who had been there. She had noticed several men she knew in the assembled company who might eventually prove to be interesting for Isabelle.

It was the end of a chapter, an era. The book of

Charlie's life had closed quietly, in a dignified manner, and as it should have, though perhaps not the warmer way he would have liked it. In spite of his sudden death, the funeral wasn't touching, and was less emotional than it should have been, but not by Isabelle's standards. She hated sloppy funerals with everyone crying and making a spectacle of themselves, and had no desire to do so herself, which wouldn't have surprised Charlie at all. Their life together wasn't tender or emotional, so why would his funeral be, entirely organized by her? Judith might have added some personal touches, but was too young to know how to do so and was always overruled by her mother. That was why she had always been closer to her father, which was so evident now.

"It was perfect in every way," Stephanie praised her. It had been better than any of Isabelle's parties, which were always perfect too. Isabelle had seen to every detail with her critical eye. She looked tired but composed as one of the servers brought them each a glass of champagne, which made it seem a bit like a celebration, but the priest who had officiated called it a celebration of life, so it was appropriate. "Charlie would have loved it," Stephanie said after a long sip. She'd been drinking champagne during the reception, but was still sober, and hungry to talk.

"No, actually, he would have hated it," Isabelle said without remorse. "He would have thought it was too formal, and he hated most of the people there, or didn't care much about them. We never liked the same people. They were mainly my friends, who came to support me. None of them knew Charlie well. He was a stickler about things like that, and always complained that things had to be 'meaningful.' I thought it was more important that it be beautiful, otherwise funerals are so depressing."

"Did you see that the Minister of the Interior was there?" Stephanie asked her. He was a very important man, handsome, but also happily married so not an appropriate target for either of the two women.

"Charlie helped him get his book published when he was in publishing. He always said he liked him, but he didn't know him that well. I'm surprised he came." There were a few important people tucked into the crowd here and there who weren't friends of Isabelle's, and who suggested a more eclectic side of Charlie which Isabelle had always chosen to ignore. She had never invited them to their parties or to the château, although she had invited the Minister of the Interior to a dinner party once. He had declined, but he came to the funeral, which would have pleased Charlie. They'd had a good rapport when the book was published. "At least we didn't have to deal with a burial," Isabelle said with relief. "My father is going to have a headstone made for our family plot, with nothing under it obviously, unless they find him. That's nice of my father, and that way I don't have to do it. I want to put this whole thing behind me now. I have to wait a while, but I want to do some house parties at the château in the fall to get things going again. I can't sit around and mourn forever," she said, sipping the champagne.

"Of course not," Stephanie seconded her. Charlie had only been dead for five days by then, and both of them would have been shocked to see him in overalls working as a car mechanic in a tiny village in Normandy only hours away. "Charlie wouldn't have expected it either." A smile crept onto Stephanie's face. "You're free now. You can do whatever you want." His will hadn't been as favorable as Isabelle had hoped, but was also typical of him. He had left their Paris apartment to the children, but Isabelle had the use of it for her lifetime, or until she remarried, so they couldn't sell it out from under her one day, and she was secure there. And fairly, which was also typical of him, he had left her the château, since he had given it to her as a gift when he bought it, to compensate her for his two difficult years of unemployment. But he had left it to her with the proviso that their children could use it freely, with their families once they had them. She wasn't thrilled about that and thought it might interfere with her at some later date, if she remarried. She had been a responsible but not warm or affectionate mother while they were growing up, and she had definite ideas about not wanting them around with their friends once they were adults. She wanted the château filled with elegant, stylish people, not her children's pals. It was not a playground for them. It was hers, more than ever now.

By law, Charlie was obliged to leave two-thirds of his fortune to their children, and instead he had left three-quarters to them, and one-quarter to Isabelle. It was going to take time now to evaluate his investment portfolio and see how to divide it between her and the children, and between Judith and Olivier. Whatever cash he had on hand was Isabelle's, and the contents of their homes were hers as well, with one exception. If there was anything the children specifically wanted, they had the right to express that to his lawyer. In all, he had divided it very fairly, with the greatest benefit to his son and daughter, but he had taken good care of Isabelle too. She wouldn't be rolling in money without his salary now, but she'd have enough income to support the château if she was careful, and she could always sell off the investments he had left her, if she needed more, and she could always marry again, or sell the château. Her lifestyle required a rich or successful man to support it, and being "careful" was unfamiliar to her, since Charlie had always indulged her in recent years to compensate her for the feelings they no longer had for each other.

Everything was about money for Isabelle. It was how she interpreted his love for her. He had respected her as his wife and the mother of his children, but even in his will, it was evident that they no longer had deep feelings for each other. He also had two life insurance policies, and had left both to his children, to help them pay for their portion of the estate taxes. He hadn't done the same for Isabelle. She would have to pay her share of taxes from what he left her, which she wasn't happy about. She had asked the attorney to make sure there wasn't a third life insurance policy, with her as beneficiary, and there wasn't. She had nothing to complain about, and no serious money worries, but he hadn't favored her over their children. As the lawyer pointed out to her, if she ever ran short of money, for whatever reason, she could sell the château to cut down on her expenses and give her a lump sum she could invest or live on. He knew from Charlie that she tended to overspend, and live above his income. She would inherit from her father one day, but there was no telling when that would be. He wasn't an old man. He was in his seventies, in good health, and although he had a large fortune, it would be cut down by inheritance taxes, and divided between her and her three sisters. Her parents might live another twenty years, so what Charlie left her was important to her. She had expected him to support her handsomely until she inherited from her parents. Given how she spent money, she wasn't feeling entirely secure after reading the will and talking to Charlie's attorney about it. Stephanie could see in her eyes that she was worried about something, and knowing her friend well, she wondered if it was about money.

"He took good care of you, I hope," she said as they finished the champagne.

"Good enough. He left as much as he could to the children, but at least I own the château."

"That's fine, if you can afford to support it."

"I'm never letting that go," Isabelle said fiercely, fire lighting her eyes, as Stephanie nodded. "The children have use of it, which could be annoying later when they're married and have children."

"It sounds like you need to take a look around at who's available, as insurance for the future," Stephanie said wisely, but as she knew only too well, rich husbands weren't easy to come by. Generous ones, who didn't have too many children. She had done well the first time, and less well the second time, with her divorces, and was still living on spousal support, with an eye out for a third husband if the opportunity presented itself. It hadn't so far. Men could see Stephanie coming. She was too obvious and had a reputation now as a gold digger, which didn't serve her well. But Isabelle was a beautiful woman, and still young enough to find a worthy husband, and she presented well as the widow of a thirty-year marriage. Her greed and extravagance were less obvious. And she had a rich father, which Stephanie didn't.

Stephanie had been a sexy young flight attendant when her first husband found her. He eventually regretted it, and left her when she tried to convince him to be less generous with his children, and to see less of them. It hadn't sat well with him, and exposed her motives to him, which others had spotted from the beginning, and he hadn't. He corrected his mistake quickly, and paid her handsomely for it, and she had rapidly gone through the money, and married again for fun and profit.

The second one was smarter, and she hadn't done as well.

Isabelle knew her history and didn't care. She was a good friend, and Isabelle had always ignored Charlie's objections to Stephanie. He thought her a bad influence, and the kind of woman he had no respect for. Isabelle was cut from the same cloth, but was more subtle about it, and had more going for her. There was a faint edge of commonness to Stephanie, which made Charlie uneasy, and none of that in Isabelle. She was well brought up and well educated.

Stephanie stayed to eat the leftovers from the reception with Isabelle, and left early. Isabelle took a long hot bath afterwards, and felt a ripple of nervousness, and anger at Charlie, as she contemplated her future. He could have done better for her, which didn't make her love him any more than she had while he was alive. In recent years, he had had no illusions about her either.

She was going to court with her lawyer in a few days to get the death certificate she had to request, so the assets he had left could be disbursed to the heirs. She had had her children sign the request too. It broke their hearts to be requesting their father's death certificate. They'd rather have had him than the money they were about to inherit. Their mother had her eye on the money more than the loss.

As Charlie worked in Armand's garage, he thought a lot about his children. He wished there were a way to let them know that he was alive, but if he did that it would defeat what he had done, stepping out of his old life, and severing his ties with it. He fully intended to go back and see his children one day. He didn't know when, and for now he didn't want to give up what he had found after the accident. It was as though he had been able to cut out the bad part of the film, the years that had gone wrong, the job he hated, which violated his principles and didn't use his intellect, the marriage that had gone sour, and the realization of what Isabelle had become, and perhaps always was. He had been able to rewind the film, and go back to a purer place where what he believed in mattered, what he needed and wanted counted, with an honorable woman he cared about and had fallen in love with, and who loved him in an honest, natural way. She was the symbol of freedom to him, the reward for the dark years of living in a loveless marriage with a woman who was incapable of loving anyone, even her own children at times, depending on her mood of the hour. They had been surrounded by people he didn't want to have in his home. Their life had been taken over by them, with a standing invitation from his wife for easy access into their life.

He had escaped a prison he had tacitly allowed himself to be led into, out of what he thought was honor. He now wondered if it had only been weakness, or cowardice, not to stand up for what he believed and wanted. He had gone along until there was no turning back. His whole adult life had been toxic. He was breathing pure air now with a woman who by sheer chance had the same values he had. He couldn't get enough of it, or of her, trying to make up for all the years before they met. Charlie thought it was worth sacrificing everything for her, the money, the property, the job, as long as the bulk of it was in his children's hands now. He had no regrets. There was not a single thing about his old life that he missed, especially now that his children were grown and gone. Every day had been a defeat for him, and a death sentence to his soul. Now he was alive again, as he had never been before, and there was no way he was going to give that up.

He and Aude talked more than he had ever talked to anyone before. They shared every moment as though it were a gift. His only identity now was his real one, the man he really was, was destined to become and never had. He got lost along the way, and now he had found himself. He felt stronger and more himself every day. He thrived with Aude, and he loved her quiet, passionate nature. She saw everything about him, even the most hidden parts, and loved him. She saw his flaws and his weaknesses and easily forgave them, and shared her own bravely. He was the only man she had ever loved and exposed herself to so freely. Charlie loved their quiet, simple life, and didn't need anything more for now. They lived on very little money, while she painted and he worked at Armand's garage and enjoyed it. He had good ideas about Armand's business and shared them with him respectfully, and Armand valued Charlie's advice and was grateful for it. He could see taking him in as a partner one day.

They stopped for a beer after work one night, and Armand asked him the question that had been troubling him. He could sense that there were secrets in Charlie's past, and even in his present. "Are you running from the law somewhere?" he finally got up the courage to ask him. Armand was a year older than Charlie, and looked twenty years older. Life had treated him harshly, along with a tendency for too much wine at night. It was how he sought oblivion and comfort before he went back to work the next day. He struggled to support his wife and four daughters, two of whom had had babies out of wedlock and lived with Armand and his wife with their children and partners. They were ten people living in a tiny four-bedroom house, with one bathroom. Nothing was easy. Charlie showed him honest ways to increase his profits. Armand tried them and found they worked. Charlie devised a simple system to keep better track of their time, so Armand billed people for the actual work he did, he didn't just guess at it and cheat himself, to their benefit. His customers were startled at first, but he did good work, and they were willing to pay for it, once they adjusted to slightly higher prices. The quality of his work saved the customers money in the long run for future car repairs. His was the best garage within a hundred miles. People knew it, and so did Armand and Charlie.

"No, I'm not running from the law," Charlie answered him, looking into his glass for a moment, remembering what he had run from. Then he looked Armand in the eyes. "I'm running from old ghosts. I was one of them. I got lost along the way. I found myself here. The past is nowhere I want to go back to. That's the only thing I'm running from." It was a fair assessment.

"You don't talk about the past. You're a smart, educated guy. You won't be happy working in a garage forever."

"I'm happy now. Happier than I've ever been. That's good enough for me. And I won't leave without giving you warning." He could tell that Armand was worried about it. He trusted him, and had started to count on him. And Charlie was scrupulously honest.

"Aude Saint-Martin is a good woman," Armand said quietly. "She came here running away too. It's been good for her."

"It's been good for me too. I like my job with you."

"You're a pretty decent mechanic." Armand smiled at him, and Charlie laughed at the grudging compliment. "I can teach you some things and make you a better one." He already had, and Charlie enjoyed the lessons. "I hope you stay," Armand said, and meant it.

"So do I. I intend to. I couldn't give this up now. A good woman, a good life, a good job. It's all I ever wanted."

"You'll find your way again. You weren't lost, you were just on a different path," Armand said philosophically. "Now that you've found the right one for you, stay on it. Don't let anyone scare you. You know what you're doing, and whatever your secrets are, they're safe with me. I don't need to know them. Show up for work, and we'll work well together." He hired Charlie for a fourth day that night, and Charlie knew he had a friend, a man of principle with a strong work ethic. He thought of

Jerome, and the differences were laughable. Everyone who knew Charlie would have been shocked to know he was working as a car mechanic in a tiny garage and liked doing it. Isabelle would have been irate if she knew. But he had left her well set with what she inherited from him, and he felt he owed her nothing now. He could do whatever he wanted. He was pretending to be dead so she and the children would get the money. It was the best he could do for them. He couldn't sell his soul and betray himself for a moment longer. He had done it for long enough.

He had let Isabelle set the bar too high and make unreasonable demands and pump him for money. He'd had to sell his soul to satisfy her. He had his soul back and he wasn't going to let anyone take it from him again. He was the master of his fate. All he wanted now was to share his life with Aude. If he lived another forty or forty-five years, if he was lucky, he wanted it to be with her. And even after a short time together, he knew it was right. He had found his destiny. He only hoped it was hers as well. Time would tell, and he had the patience to wait and find out. He wasn't in a hurry. He wasn't rushing anywhere. He had time. And so did she. She saw it the same way he did.

He went home to her after his beer with Armand, having put his employer's fears to rest. She was waiting for him when he got home. She had just stepped out of the shower after a long day's work at her easel, and she stood there naked and spectacularly beautiful, and smiled at him. He wanted to remember the moment forever, as he walked toward her, took her in his arms, and buried the past again.

Chapter 7

As time passed, Isabelle's mood shifted from shock to anger at Charlie for leaving more to the children than he had to, for giving them the Paris apartment, even if she had lifetime use of it if she didn't remarry, for giving them free access to the château for their lifetimes. Even if they were her children too, she didn't want them there one day with spouses and children. She was angry at him for letting them pick what they wanted from their family homes. Judith had chosen a painting she had always loved, which was valuable, and two small sculptures by Rodin that were models for his larger work. Isabelle was angry at Charlie for everything the children had gotten and she hadn't, no matter how much he had left her. And most of all, she was angry at him for dying. Overnight he had cast her into a pool of middle-aged and older women who found themselves single again and were desperate for husbands, and now had to compete with girls in their twenties and thirties, the age of her own daughter.

Isabelle wasn't desperate, but she was eager to find a man who would support her to the extreme degree she wanted. So far she hadn't seen a single one. It was hard enough finding available, unattached men for dinner parties, let alone to marry. And it was obvious that Isabelle was expensive. Stephanie had the same problem, but at least Isabelle came equipped with a château in excellent condition, thanks to Charlie, a fashionable Paris apartment, an impressive wardrobe, and the investment portfolio Charlie had left her. But all any of that did was attract all the fortune hunters in Paris who were targeting women her age and older. There wasn't a real eligible bachelor in the bunch. She'd had dates with three of them, and they were so blatant she stopped taking their calls.

"What a sorry lot they are," she complained to Stephanie, who knew the options well, and had dated several of the same men. But Isabelle spotted them quickly, just as others did with her. Socially, in those circles, Paris was a small city, and had few secrets. Isabelle wasn't a welcome offering in the marketplace. The married women she knew were wary of her, with good reason. She considered married men fair game too, if she could get them away from their wives. She had few scruples when it came to improving her lot in life, and she felt she deserved it, just as she felt she deserved more than Charlie had given her, and ultimately left her when he died.

"It's a bitch, isn't it?" Stephanie said, and Isabelle agreed. She couldn't even spend whatever she wanted at Hermès and Chanel anymore, since she was the one paying the bills, and if she spent too much it would eventually come out of her investments. The realities had begun to hit home within weeks after Charlie died. She kept busy and didn't miss him, and had resumed her social life very quickly. She had no time to waste. She was on a mission. She was giving house parties at the château every weekend to compensate for the fact that she was getting fewer invitations from married women. She was a threat now. And the competition was stiff with forty-year-old divorcees, fifty- and sixty-year-old widows, the even more desperate older ones, and especially the beautiful single girls in their twenties and thirties.

Isabelle had thought of divorcing Charlie from time to time, thinking she could do better, but had had no idea what she'd be facing. She had a full view of it now, and was inviting every worthwhile bachelor in Paris to her château weekends. And in fact, the men had the pick of the litter. There were far fewer eligible men than women, and only a few of the men were desperate. They were the ones she didn't want.

She discovered that many of them were discreetly gay, which was of no interest to her either. She wanted a husband with a great deal of money, and then what Charlie had left her would just be gravy, instead of the main meal. His death had turned out to be not only unfortunate and premature, but financially alarming, which was just what she'd been afraid of when he died. She was still a lot better off than Stephanie, but Isabelle set her sights a lot higher, and thought she deserved more and had more to offer.

Stephanie was a few years older, and not as attractive, and came without real estate or investments. And divorce still bore a stigma in France, while being a widow didn't. But no one observing her would have thought that Isabelle was in deep mourning for her husband. She missed him occasionally, but not often, and the rest of the time she was angry, although she was smart enough to conceal it. Only Stephanie knew the truth, and how bitter and angry she was. Her longtime lack of love for him had turned to deep resentment. It gave her a hard expression, and an unhappy frown that even Botox couldn't erase. She thought it was stupid and irresponsible of him to drive to the château late at night when he was tired, and go off the road, either not paying close enough attention or falling asleep at the wheel. He had made her life uncomfortable instead of carefree as before. She loved her freedom now, and the men it had brought into her life.

She didn't miss Charlie, but she missed the status and security being married to him gave her. And instead of grief softening her, anger had hardened her, and it showed. It was all she could do not to speak ill of him when people offered their condolences.

At the end of September, Charlie had been gone for three months. It had been a summer of bliss and love with Aude like nothing he had ever known. They spent long loving nights together, made love whenever they wanted. She had done some of her best paintings, including a portrait of him she thought was her best work, and she wasn't going to sell it.

They went for walks and swam. He took her fishing. They drove deeper into Normandy on weekends, stayed at small inns, and discovered beaches and coves she had never seen before. Every moment seemed idyllic, and they basked in the warmth of their love for each other.

His wounds from the accident had long since healed, with the exception of two small scars on his face, and one ugly one on his arm he didn't care about. Aude stopped worrying that she would come home one day and find him gone, back to his old life. He still spoke of seeing his children again, but he couldn't find a way to do so now, without endangering the life he had built, and as the inheritances would have been distributed by then, it would have been legally complicated to return from the dead and admit he was alive. In effect, he had done what he claimed others did, he had walked out of his life and, in a different place, had begun a whole new life. He didn't miss the old one, especially his wife.

It was almost as though the past had never existed. He had been reborn, and preferred everything about his life now, and most of all the woman he loved. He wished he had found her sooner, and could erase the past, except for his children. But there was no way he could have pieces of his past life while embracing his new one. His heart was with Aude, and where he was now.

They had devised a system where Armand paid him in cash at the garage, and Charlie kept the money in a locked drawer in Aude's cabin. He had long since repaid her for what she had advanced him in the beginning, and he paid for everything now from their cash drawer. Her money from the gallery was her own. With the simple life they led, he was well able to pay for their needs with his earnings from the garage. He was continuing to help Armand make changes that made his business more profitable. He had even spent a weekend helping him clean the place up. They had repainted it, and replaced a few things, and Aude had made them bright new signs that looked terrific. Armand had already spoken of making him a partner, but

Charlie was happy as an employee, and doing what he could for him. Armand had even encouraged his two unmarried daughters with children to move out, so his living situation had improved. Charlie was proving to be a blessing in the life of those he touched, particularly Aude.

"You know, you won't be happy until you go back to Paris, tell them the truth, and clean things up," she said to him one day, as they lay in the soft grass near a stream on one of their long walks in the countryside.

"I'm happy now," he said peacefully. "And that would be a mess." He didn't mind their thinking he was dead. Materially, it had benefited them, and he loved his freedom and life with her.

"You're too honest to do this forever," she said.

"Maybe I'm not." He had discovered things about himself in the past months that he had never realized before. He had time for introspection here, both when he was working at the garage and with her. He had the gift of time, as well as the gift of love. "Besides, I like being dead. It keeps things simple," he teased her, put an arm around her and kissed her. "I understand now why people do something like this. It was the best decision I ever made, and I'm happy with you." He realized that if he hadn't met her, he probably would have gone back.

"I love you, and I think it will haunt you later," she predicted.

"Can we worry about it then?" he asked her,

tickling her neck with a blade of grass. There was a lighthearted feeling to his life now that he hadn't had since he was a boy.

"If you wait years, your children will never forgive you for abandoning them for so long. It's only months now." She was worried about it, for his sake, knowing how much he loved them.

"Are you trying to get rid of me?"

"No, I just don't want you to have regrets later."

"I have no regrets. I'm happy with my life with you. It's all I want. I've been living for other people for thirty years. Now it's my turn."

"You don't have to be dead to do that. You can set better boundaries, find a new job, and get a divorce."

"I was more generous in my will than I would have been in a divorce. She won't want to change that now, and I'm sure she's very happy as a widow. I'm certain she'll remarry in no time."

"And then she'll be a bigamist, without even knowing."

"I'm fine with that. The only problem really is that I can't marry you, because I am married, and I'd like to marry you one day."

"I don't need to be married. I've been married. I'm much more married to you."

"Me too. So that settles it. I'm staying dead." He wasn't in the mood to be serious about it, and they got back in the car and drove home via a leisurely route as the day got cooler. Their time together always seemed precious and like a special gift, to both of them.

A month later, the air was chilly and fall was in the air. The cabin seemed cozier in the cool weather, and Charlie lit a fire at night to keep the living room warm. They had to be more careful on their walks. The hunters had come out, and they heard gunshots occasionally. Charlie had no interest in hunting. It had never been a sport which attracted him, and Aude didn't like guns either. Isabelle's father loved hunting and went on fancy shoots with his friends all over Europe. He had invited Charlie several times and he always declined. Shooting a bunch of birds out of the sky seemed pointless to him, as did freezing in a duck blind. And shooting bigger game seemed cruel to him.

Charlie and Aude had just gone to bed one night and were cuddling in the chilly room. The fire had gone out in the living room fireplace, and Aude didn't like space heaters, because she thought they were dangerous. She had a fear of fires because of how her parents had died. So they were holding each other close for warmth, and Charlie had just started to make love to her, when they heard shots ring out not too far away. They both jumped, and Charlie didn't like how close the shots were to the house. He wondered if it was a couple of teenagers with their fathers' guns, which he didn't like either.

"Do they hunt at night?" he asked her, startled.

"I don't think so. I'm sure they're not supposed

to." They listened for a while and there were no further shots. They relaxed and made love and fell asleep. At four in the morning they woke with a start, and heard another round of shots, a little farther away this time. Charlie lay in bed listening, then got up and locked the door. Aude waited for him to come back to bed, and wrapped her arms around him again.

"It's nothing. Go back to sleep, it's just hunters. They do that at this time of year." They were both asleep again five minutes later, and the rest of the night was peaceful.

Charlie mentioned it at breakfast the next morning. "I don't like that. They were too close to the house. And random shooting like that can be dangerous. They might even have been drunk."

"They do it every year. It's harmless. They shoot rabbits and small animals and birds. They've never shot a person in the eight years I've lived here."

"I'm very happy having people think I'm dead, but I don't want some local hunter making an honest man of me, or shooting you. Do you think we should report it to the police?"

"They know about it. There's nothing they can do. Once in a while they actually shoot someone's dog, and all hell breaks loose. And then they do it again next year. We just can't go walking in the woods for a while, until hunting season is over. But if we stay in the open and they see us, no one is going to shoot us," she said, unworried, as Charlie got ready to leave for work.

"I have to replace a transmission today," he said, looking distracted, and then he smiled. It was a far cry from board meetings and new product presentations to the sales force, or meetings with government regulatory agencies. He was changing transmissions and replacing brakes, and he didn't mind at all. He loved it, and all the time he had to spend with her. He didn't miss his other life, only his kids. He smiled thinking about how outraged Isabelle would have been if she'd known she was married to a car mechanic, with hands black with grease and oil by the end of the day, working in overalls like a common laborer. That's what he was now, and he didn't mind it. He had never imagined following a path like this, but it had turned out to be just what he needed. There were no further gunshots that night, or for the next few days.

Isabelle gave a weekend house party that weekend. She tried out a new chef and he was even better than the one she'd been using. She had eighteen people staying at the château, and had invited several new people she had met recently, trying to broaden her social circle so she would get invited to more parties herself. Her social life had slowed down over the summer, with many people away, and others feeling it was too soon to invite her after her husband's untimely death, and hostesses who weren't keen to invite her now as a single woman. A single woman was considered a pariah by most hostesses, while a single man was seen as a prize. The realities of single life.

To see her charming her guests, and flitting around among them, no one would have thought she was recently bereaved and had lost her husband only four months before.

"She's a brave girl," one of her guests whispered as they watched her smiling and laughing with one of two single men invited for the weekend. "She puts a good face on it, while her heart must be breaking." Stephanie overheard them and knew just how far from the truth it was. Isabelle was relieved to be free now, in spite of her concerns about her future, and her fear of running out of money eventually. She had to be more careful now than she had been when Charlie was alive, and she resented him bitterly for that. His death had been upsetting, inconvenient, and unnecessary if he hadn't undertaken a winding road when he was tired after a long day and a possibly stressful meeting.

Losing Charlie had jangled her considerably, but it hadn't broken her heart, and the silver lining for her was the freedom she had now, to see, entertain, or date whomever she wanted. Just as it was for Charlie, for Isabelle it was an unexpected release from the prison of their loveless marriage, which wasn't entirely a bad thing for either of them. Charlie would have agreed with her on that.

A week after the first time they heard shots in the night, Aude and Charlie heard them again. They were closer to the house this time, and seemed louder. Charlie wanted to go outside and give a shout, and Aude told him not to. She didn't want a stray bullet to hit him, especially if the shooter was drunk, which seemed like a likely possibility at that hour. It was three A.M. The village where she lived was a peaceful community, and violence there was unheard of. There had been a nasty domestic situation several years back, where a man had killed his wife in a jealous rage and then committed suicide. He had caught her in bed with his brother, and it had turned the local residents upside down for a while, but it was a case of domestic violence, not a random crime.

Aude was sure that this was just the usual hunters, drunk or overexcited, with no criminal intention or harm to any human involved. Charlie didn't like it anyway, and told her to be careful when she left the house. She calmed him down again, and he mentioned it at the garage the next day. Armand confirmed what Aude had said, that it happened every year, a flurry of gunshots here and there, and no one had ever gotten hurt as a result.

Charlie believed what they both said, but he

didn't like sloppy behavior with firearms, however random and benign the intentions. He and Aude stopped going for walks in the evenings, in the crisp October air, and the next time they heard the shots, Charlie didn't get out of bed. He had taken to locking the door every night ever since it started, just to be on the safe side. The third time, he thought nothing of it, turned over in bed, and went back to sleep.

In the morning, when he left for work, he found three dead squirrels on their doorstep and a skinned rabbit. Someone had left them there intentionally. Was it a prank or a warning? He wasn't sure. Aude was standing just behind him, and when he turned to look at her, her face was sheet white.

Chapter 8

Aude looked like she was going to faint when she saw the dead animals on her doorstep. Charlie told her to go back inside, disposed of them in the forest nearby, then came back to wash his hands and talk to her. She was waiting in the kitchen, at the table, her legs too shaky to hold her.

"Is that usual at this time of year too?" The skinned rabbit was the most disturbing. Aude shook her head in answer.

"I don't think so. Maybe the person shooting last night was drunk or crazy. No one's ever done that before," she admitted.

"I'm going to tell the police, or maybe you should." His situation without proper ID papers was sketchy, and he didn't want to draw attention to himself, or have to explain why he didn't have any, since he was presumed to be dead and wanted to stay that way. He had taken to using part of her last name locally, calling himself Charles Martin. No one had questioned him so far, and beyond her community, people who didn't know them assumed that they were married when they saw them together. They looked like any other ordinary couple, despite the seventeen-year difference in their ages. Charlie was still wearing his wedding ring out of habit, and looked youthful enough for their being together to seem reasonable. "I suppose I shouldn't go to the police myself," he reconsidered, and she looked at him with worried eyes, although there was color in her face again. "Do you know who might have left the dead animals on the doorstep?" As he sat across the kitchen table from her, he suddenly had the distinct impression that she did. He didn't like the look on her face. She looked terrified, as though she'd seen a ghost. He hadn't forgotten what she'd told him about her ex-husband. Plenty of people in Charlie's previous life cheated on each other, even in his milieu, but they didn't commit crimes like that. They just weren't violent about it. "Could it have anything to do with your ex-husband?"

"I haven't heard from him in eight years. He's never tried to contact me since the divorce, and he still has several years to serve in prison, two more years, or longer. I know he can't be out now. But he had a passion for guns, and he liked to hunt small animals with them, even as a boy. He told me so.

And he liked to skin them. I saw him do it once and it was awful. It looked just like the rabbit on our doorstep this morning. He's the only person I know who would do a thing like that. It was like a signature and a reminder to me that he's still alive somewhere."

"It could have been any boy or man in the neighborhood." Charlie tried to reassure her. "If he's still in prison, it wasn't him," he said calmly. "He's not the first man to kill some squirrels and skin a rabbit. It's probably just coincidence."

"I don't think so," she said with huge frightened eyes. "I think it's him, and he wanted me to know that he's around."

"There's a simple solution to that, or there should be. Can you check to see if he's still in prison, without his knowing?"

"I'm not sure. I think so."

"Does he know where you live?"

She nodded. "My address was on the divorce papers. I'll see what I can find out today," she said. "And Charlie, I'm sorry." The last thing she wanted was to bring her past into Charlie's life, or put him in danger, or herself.

"It doesn't matter. He'd probably have found out about me sooner or later, if he has your address. And we have nothing to hide, or at least you don't." He smiled at her. "You're divorced, and a free woman. As for me, I'm officially dead, which could be a problem." He smiled and tried to cheer her up. He could see how worried she was.

"He's insanely jealous. I don't want him to hurt you," she said, as her eyes filled with tears. For her, it was a replay of what had led up to her lover's death eight years before. "I don't see how he could have gotten out. Paul was sentenced to a minimum of ten years in prison for Jean-Michel's death." Charlie didn't need to ask her who that was. He could guess it was the man she'd been dating after she and her husband separated.

"Let's find out where he is," Charlie said, "and then, if necessary, you can go to the police and report the incident." He left for work a little while later, telling her to lock the door behind him and to let him know what she found out.

She waited another hour, then called the prison. The last she knew of Paul, he was at the Réau prison. She still had his prison number written down, and all the pertinent information. When she called, hoping to get information more easily, she said she was his wife, and they connected her to his caseworker. Aude assumed he was still incarcerated at Réau, a maximum-security prison.

After a long wait, the caseworker, Virgil Thomas, came on the line. He wanted to know who she was and why she was inquiring about Paul Pasquier. She repeated that she was his wife, and he told her in a stern tone that the inmate in question was divorced. She corrected it to ex-wife then and asked if Paul was still in prison or if he'd been released. There was a long pause, and Virgil Thomas spoke to her coldly.

"Pasquier escaped ten days ago," he said, and Aude caught her breath when she heard the words. "Do you have information about his whereabouts?" She described the shots she'd heard at night, and the dead squirrels and rabbit on her doorstep.

"They could have been left by anyone." Virgil Thomas wasn't impressed.

"He liked skinning animals," she said meekly. "It worried me that he might be free now, which is why I called." He asked for her name, address, and phone number, which she gave him, and told her to call if she had any further information or heard from Paul Pasquier. She was convinced now that it was him, and felt panic tighten her throat.

"It's not adequate evidence to convince me it's Pasquier," the caseworker told her in a slightly warmer tone, "but it's certainly a possibility, particularly if he is still angry with you about the divorce. Be very careful," he warned her. "Do you live alone?"

"I . . . uh . . . no, I don't." She stumbled over the words, and he told her that the authorities considered Pasquier dangerous. He had another fifteen years to serve now, after killing a fellow prisoner three years before. "He had been moved to a medium security area of the prison for the remainder of his sentence, and got in a fight." Virgil Thomas urged her again to be careful, and to advise the police or the prison if she saw her ex-husband. "We assume he's armed, and we know he's dangerous. Use extreme caution," he said seriously, concerned after talking to her.

"Thank you," she said, and hung up with a shaking hand. She called Charlie at the garage immediately and told him what she'd heard. He told her to stay inside, keep the doors and windows locked, and he'd come home at lunchtime to discuss it with her.

He explained to Armand that he had to leave for a few hours, and knocked on the cabin door shortly before noon. She approached the door with caution, and let Charlie in when she saw it was him. He looked as worried as she did, and they sat down to discuss what to do next. She was sure now that her ex-husband was in the area, and had left the dead animals on her doorstep as a warning, to frighten her. She told Charlie that the caseworker had told her he'd alert the local police.

"You need to get out of here," Charlie told her firmly. "You can't sit here waiting for him to show up. If he was the one shooting, he's been around here for more than a week, and he came right up to the door last night. He's probably seen us," Charlie said, worried about her.

She sighed when he said it. She was sure he was right. "Maybe the timing is right," she said softly.

"To get killed?" Charlie said to her. "I hope not.

I want you away from here, Aude, as fast as we can arrange it."

"I think you should go home," she said. "You've been gone for more than four months. Your children deserve to know you're alive. The idea of walking away from your life is a nice fantasy, but in reality you have responsibilities. You can't run away from them forever. You need to make a clean break before we can have a life."

He knew it was true but had been trying to avoid it. At some point, being a "dead man" would become increasingly complicated. He'd discovered what he needed to know about himself, and his marriage, and even his job. He had Aude now. He wanted a real life with her, to live with her openly and not in hiding. And maybe even marriage and children one day, although he hadn't asked her, and there was no rush to decide. In their minds, they felt as good as married now. But the reality was something different, and masquerading as a dead man had its disadvantages. It would take some serious help to reverse what he'd done, pay back insurance payments that had been distributed, and unsnarl the mess that had probably been created with taxes. But he knew Aude was right. He owed it to his children to go back and clean up the mess, relieve their minds, and face Isabelle. Isabelle would have to return any pension she'd gotten. And he owed Jerome an explanation too, and wanted to leave his job properly.

"Charlie, you have to leave now," Aude said urgently. "I'm sure he's seen us, and if he knows you're with me, he'll kill you. He did it before. You're in more danger than I am. He's crazy."

"I believe you, but I'm not leaving you here. I can resurface any time in my life. I want you away from here as fast as we can get you out."

"To where? This is my home. It's where I work. I have nowhere else to go."

"We'll get you a place where he can't find you."

"What if he's watching us now?" She looked terrified, and Charlie was trying not to catch her panic. It was contagious.

"If he were, he'd be knocking on the door. Let's try to stay calm. We'll get you a little cottage somewhere, and when you're settled, I'll go to Paris and deal with things there. It'll take a while to sort out the technicalities. I don't want to drag you into my mess. We'll find a quiet place and rent you a house, and when you feel safe there, I'll deal with Paris. They've lived without me for this long, they'll survive a few more weeks before I return. You're the most important now. I want to get you out of here quickly."

"When?" Her eyes were huge and frightened.

"Tonight, if we can. Or at worst, tomorrow."

"I can't leave that fast," she said, looking around, and he held her hand.

"Yes, you can. Your safety means everything to me. He's not expecting us to leave. He's probably not watching us that closely, if he is at all. You start packing. I'll go and talk to Armand. I hate to leave him without notice, but I don't think we have much choice." She nodded, and went to pull out a suitcase. Then she turned to Charlie again.

"What'll I do with my paintings?"

"Leave them here for now. We'll come back once they've caught him. You said they're looking for him now. I'm sure they want to catch him as soon as they can. We'll come back here later, for the rest of your things, or if you want to stay here."

She looked at Charlie. "You said 'you.' You won't come back with me?" She wondered how much of his life he was going back to and if he was going to stay. She could feel him slipping away from her, and it frightened her almost as much as her ex-husband finding them. She didn't want to lose Charlie, but she knew that if his decision was to go back to his old life, she couldn't stop him. Maybe it had all been a fantasy, a dream they had lived for a short time, and now it was over. He saw the look on her face and pulled her gently into his arms.

"I'm not leaving you, Aude. I'm straightening things out for us. If it weren't for you, I'd never go back. I'd just keep hiding and running. But you deserve better than that, and you're right about my children too. I took the fast, easy way out when I had the chance. Now I have to do it right, for all our sakes. Wherever you are, I'll come and be with you. I can go back and forth until I clean things up properly. I'm not abandoning you, but I do want to get you to safety." She nodded and wiped the tears from her eyes.

He reminded her to lock up and draw the curtains, and he left to see Armand. He hated to give him bad news, but if her ex-husband was in the area, and watching them, there was no way he could be sure that Aude would be safe, unless he removed her as rapidly as possible. They were sitting ducks in her cabin at night if it really was Pasquier shooting in the vicinity. Charlie was more than willing to believe that Paul was crazy, if he had already killed two men now. That was proof enough for Charlie. He wanted to get Aude as far as he could from any danger.

He explained the whole story to Armand when he got to the garage, and his would-be partner looked at him sadly.

"You're leaving now?"

Charlie nodded.

"I think we have to. Her ex-husband is dangerous. He's an escaped convict now, and a murderer. And she thinks he's around here somewhere."

"Then you're right to go. Do you think you'll come back here to live after they send him back to prison?" He looked momentarily hopeful.

"I don't know," Charlie was honest with him. "My life is complicated at the moment too. I have some things I need to clean up and get in order. The car they brought you that the Coast Guard found fifteen meters down was mine. I went over the cliff that night, and somehow survived it. I have to go back and do things right now. I have grown children who still need a father. I've had four months here that have been the best of my life, and I've loved working with you. I won't forget that."

"If you come back, I'll make you my partner in the garage," Armand said with a warm smile. The two men were friends now, and respected each other.

"It's the best job I've had in years. And you taught me a lot."

"You taught me some things too. You're a good man to work with. A good man all around. Take care of yourself, and come back when you're ready. The garage and I will be waiting for you."

"You'll see me again," Charlie promised, and meant it.

"Now get the hell out of town, before that asshole finds you," Armand said, and Charlie smiled.

"Take care, my friend." Charlie patted Armand on the shoulder and left with a heavy heart to go back to Aude's cottage. The months with Armand had been good ones. It was genuine work, and he had earned his money and enjoyed working with him. He hated to leave now, but it was the right thing to do.

Aude let him in when he knocked on the door, and she had three packed suitcases waiting and ready. She had packed another bag with his things.

She had carefully covered her paintings with linen and plastic, and had neatly stacked them against each other in the kitchen. There were at least twenty she hadn't sent to her gallery yet and still wanted to add last touches to. Her paints were neatly arranged on a table. She had packed a sketchpad and some pencils. The house looked tidy, and she was wearing jeans, a white sweater, and a warm jacket. Charlie looked around the cottage where they had been so happy and it had all started.

"We'll be back," he promised, and hugged her, and then he went to load the car as quickly as he could so no one would notice. He didn't have the feeling that anyone was around, but they couldn't be sure. She locked the cabin while he waited in the car, thinking of the first time he'd seen it, the lights glowing through the trees as he stumbled through the woods, and she opened the door, and magic happened.

The car was running when she got in, and they headed down the dirt road. She had brought some things to eat and had thrown out the rest, and she looked at him. Everything had happened so fast. But if Paul Pasquier was anywhere in the vicinity, they needed to go. It was the smart thing to do.

"Where are we going?" she asked him.

"I have absolutely no idea," he said, as he turned onto the road in the direction he had come from on the night of the accident. Ultimately, in two hours it would lead them to Paris, but there were many other options before that. He knew the area fairly well and could think of some places where she would be comfortable and safe while she waited for him. It felt like an adventure to both of them, and Aude already looked better as the village where she had lived for eight years shrank behind them, and they put some distance between them and where they feared now that her ex-husband might be hiding. It was a while before they saw another village, and quite a distance before they saw a town, as they drove along beside the ocean. They had passed the place where he had driven off the cliff, and he recognized it, and glanced at Aude.

"This is where it all started, four and a half months ago. It feels like a lifetime." She nodded and leaned over to kiss him. It was quite a distance to the next village, and he traveled the familiar road he used to take to and from the château. He was driving her banged-up car, but had recently given it a tune-up, new brakes, and new tires, and it felt like new.

They stopped for dinner at a beach town he had never been to before, Équemauville. It was a little harbor town, with a quaint main street, and twelve hundred residents. It was four times the population of Vattetot. There was a small hotel, and Charlie booked a room for the night. On the way to dinner, he noticed a realtor's office, with photographs of several cottages for rent that looked pretty. They

were less than an hour from where she'd been living, and it was more of a summer beach community, but it was more populated, which he liked
better for her. He didn't want to leave her in some
deserted place where no one would be nearby to
help her, while he was in Paris, straightening things
out.

They had a good dinner, and then went to the
hotel. The room he'd rented was small and cozy
with a fireplace, and they went to bed and he held
her. He knew she was still nervous about the future, and her ex-husband, but she was safe here,
and Charlie liked the feel of the little town. It
seemed friendly, and there were shops and a few
restaurants, and a famous church and convent
where a saint had lived in the religious life, which
seemed like a good sign to Charlie.

They locked the door to their room, and both of
them slept well, without worrying about gunshots
in the night and criminal ex-husbands. Their rapid
exit from her cottage had rattled them, and they
felt safe in the little town where they spent the
night. It was so picturesque. It was hard to imagine
anything bad happening there, on brightly lit
streets with houses, restaurants, and stores nearby.
No one suspicious could lurk around without being
noticed.

They had a breakfast of croissants and café au
lait at the hotel and walked down to the realtor's

office afterwards. The woman who ran it explained that it was more of a summer community, and their rentals were available at a reduced rate in the winter. They had five available at the moment. The others were used by their owners on winter weekends. Aude was shocked when she heard the prices, even at the winter rate, and shook her head at Charlie. She was sure they could find something cheaper, but he insisted he wanted to see them. He was on his way back to real life with a bank account and credit cards, although for the moment it all belonged to his wife and children. But he intended to reclaim at least some of it to live on. And he could easily afford any of the houses they were about to show him. Aude had never had a clear picture of what he had, or had left behind, and didn't want to know, but she had a sudden impression that it was more than she had guessed. He had never told her about the château in Veules-les-Roses. He was modest and discreet and it hadn't dawned on her that he might be wealthy. She loved his heart and soul, she wasn't after money.

Two of the houses looked depressing to both of them. The third one was a large old-fashioned family home, with much more space and more bedrooms than they needed. And two were quaint cottages, in good condition, which would be pleasant for her to live in, while she waited to go home to her cabin with him. He picked the one he could tell she liked best and rented it on a month-to-month basis. They both hoped that it wouldn't be long until Paul Pasquier returned to prison and she was out of danger. Once he was in custody again, she could go back to her cabin to wait for Charlie to finish his business of returning to the land of the living, reclaiming some of his money, and filing for divorce.

"You can occupy it immediately," the realtor told them. Charlie had to rely on Aude, as he had in the beginning, to write a check for the month's rent and a deposit, and promised to pay her back as soon as he had a bank account again, in a matter of days. They went to check out of the hotel then, and came back with their bags and the keys to the cottage. Charlie carried her things in for her, and set them down in the bedroom she intended to use, with a view of the ocean, as she looked at him, worried.

"Isn't this much too expensive?" she asked him, feeling guilty, and he smiled at her.

"I can manage it." They went to buy groceries then and filled the fridge. The cottage had kitchen utensils, and linens, a TV in the living room and a stereo system. It was much fancier than her cabin in the woods, and she giggled as she discovered its different features and tried them all.

"I've never had a house as fancy as this," she said. Charlie thought of the château that Isabelle had inherited by now, and that he was going to give her in the divorce. It was a far cry from this summer cottage, and Aude was more grateful than Isabelle had ever been. They went to bed early that night and made love. The cottage had an impersonal feeling to it, with none of their things around, but they were starting to feel at home there. Anywhere he was with her felt like home to him now.

They went for a long walk on the beach the next morning and came back to the house so he could make the call he had avoided for four months and thought he'd never make again. He didn't call Isabelle, which was too big of a jump. He called his lawyer. When he said his name, Philippe Delacroix's secretary put him through immediately.

"Who is this?" the lawyer asked in a harsh tone, expecting to hear an imposter claiming to be Charlie. He recognized his voice an instant later.

"It's me, Philippe, Charlie."

"Oh my God," the lawyer said, profoundly shaken. "What happened? Where've you been? I went to your funeral."

"I know. It's a long story," Charlie said, holding Aude's hand. She was worried too. "I'll tell you when I see you."

"Where are you now?"

"About an hour and a half outside Paris." *With the love of my life,* he wanted to add, but didn't. Philippe would have a lot to absorb when he saw him. He realized from Philippe's surprised tone that his reappearance would be shocking.

"Have you been in a hospital all this time?"

"No, I haven't," Charlie said quietly.

"Have you called Isabelle?"

"No, I called you first."

"You'd better come to my office before you go home."

"Is she remarried yet?" Charlie asked, only half joking. Anything was possible. He knew her well.

"Of course not. But we all believed you died, and things were handled accordingly. There's going to be a lot of administrative work to do now that you're back."

"I figured that would be the case. I almost didn't come back," he said, "but it wouldn't be fair to the kids. And I miss them. How are they?"

"Fine, as far as I know." Charlie didn't ask about his wife. He would see her soon enough, and he could guess that she wouldn't be happy to see him after almost five months. She'd be worried about the money that might not be hers now. But he intended to be generous with her, which she didn't know. "When are you coming back to the city?"

"Today," Charlie said with a sigh, and a longing look at Aude. He didn't want to go back at all, but he knew he had to, for his kids' sake, and maybe for his own. Aude was right. He needed to do this honestly, and cleanly. She had said that all along, and known that he'd want to. Running away and hiding had been easier than going back would be now. But he was ready. He'd been thinking about it for a while. Paul Pasquier just speeded up the timing.

"Come to the office when you get here," Philippe said firmly. "And Charlie," he said, with emotion in his voice, "welcome back. I've missed you." Whatever Charlie had been doing, Philippe was glad he was alive.

"You might be the only one," Charlie commented, touched that his lawyer, who was also his friend, actually cared about him and was happy he was back. Other than his children, Charlie suspected Philippe might be the only person he knew who would be genuinely happy to see him.

Aude knew when he hung up that he was leaving. He promised her he would be back soon. He would come and stay for a few days whenever he could, while he was working things out. They had cell phones so she could call him, and he'd call her, and he promised to work everything out as quickly as he could. He told her to call the police if she saw her ex or suspected he was in the vicinity. In the end, there was nothing left to say. They made love one last time, and she stood on the steps and waved as he drove away in a car he had rented that day, so he could leave Aude's car with her. It was the end of a chapter in their lives, and they both knew that it would never be quite the same as when they had been alone in her cozy cabin in a world all their own. There would be other people in their lives in the future. But for now, they still had each other in their own private universe, and whatever lay ahead, they knew they would be together. But he had to make amends to his children, and there would be dragons to slay.

Chapter 9

There was more traffic than he expected, when Charlie drove into the city. It took him almost two hours to get there. And when he saw the familiar city where he had lived all his life, it took his breath away. He forgot sometimes how beautiful Paris was and how much he loved it. When he crossed the Champs-Élysées, he looked toward the Arc de Triomphe with the enormous French flag flying under the arch, and it brought tears to his eyes. He was home.

He drove to his lawyer's office on the rue François Premier, in the 8th Arrondissement. Some of the most elegant shops in Paris were there. It reminded him of Isabelle, as he took the elevator to his lawyer's office. Philippe Delacroix came out to the reception area immediately and hugged him, and looked very emotional. Charlie followed him back to his private office, where he'd been a hundred times. Philippe was younger than Charlie, but not by much. Philippe was married for the second time, and had had two children with each wife.

He waved Charlie to a chair, and sat across his desk from him, looking him over carefully. Charlie looked well and happy and relaxed, and Philippe guessed immediately that there was a woman involved. But this was clearly a bigger story than that. Charlie had been believed dead for almost five months, a long time to just disappear from your life and let your loved ones think you died. Clearly, he had changed his mind if he was back.

"What happened?" Philippe asked Charlie, who wondered where to start.

"I had an accident. I've been thinking of telling Isabelle and my kids that I hit my head and lost my memory, but that's not right. I came back to settle things and tell the truth. I was tired, it was late, it's a bad road on the way to the château. I fell asleep at the wheel, went over a cliff, and got banged up pretty badly. I don't know how, but the car door opened, and I got out. The car sank after I got out. I made it to the surface, and clawed my way up the cliff, got to the road and started walking. And as I did, I realized that it was the perfect opportunity to walk out of my life and never come back, to let everyone think I was dead. I hated my life." He didn't say he had almost let himself drown, and initially his survival had been purely instinctive.

"You decided that before anything else happened, before you met anyone?" Philippe asked him, and Charlie nodded.

"I hated everything about my life, my job for that asshole Jansen, my marriage, the château, the people she filled it with every weekend. I hated all of it. My life had no meaning I cared about. I thought of letting myself drown too, but I didn't," he admitted then. "I just wanted to run away forever and never come back. The accident was my chance to escape. I'd never realized before how much I wanted to. So I seized it. I started to drive to the château the next day, and I just couldn't do it."

"People have done it and never been found again," Philippe commented, impressed by what he'd heard so far.

"Our marriage had been dead for years. I knew Isabelle wouldn't give a damn if I died, or might even prefer it. I can't even remember when we loved each other. Anyway, I walked after the accident, and didn't see a house or a person or a car for at least an hour. Then I saw a small cabin lit up in the forest. I got to the door on my last legs by then, and a woman opened it. She changed my life. She's beautiful and smart and loving. She's a painter, studied at the Beaux-Arts. She's incredible. We've been together since that night, living in her cabin, while I worked as a car mechanic, which I loved by the way. She always said that I should come back for the kids and she was right, so here I am. And I know this is going to be a huge mess for you to sort out."

"Where is she now? Did you bring her with you?" Philippe hoped not, but you never knew. It would make everything that much harder if he did. But Charlie was smarter than that, and he wanted to protect Aude too.

"No, I came alone. I need to take care of business by myself."

"What do you want? To go back to Isabelle?" It didn't sound like it, but he was an honorable man, sometimes too much so, to his own detriment. And Philippe noticed he still wore his wedding ring.

"No, of course not. We should have ended it years ago. I want a divorce. She can keep the château I left her in my will. I want the use of the apartment, instead of her having it, but I want to leave ownership of the apartment to my kids, as it was in my will. The only thing I want back from the kids is this: I gave them seventy-five percent of my assets and investments, instead of the sixty-six percent prescribed by law. They can keep the sixty-six percent, but I'd like the nine-percent difference back. I'll live on that. Whatever pension Isabelle got from Jansen she needs to return, since I'm not dead. And we'll have to give back the insurance money I had designated to pay the inheritance taxes, but the state will have to give us back the taxes also, since I'm not dead, so that goes back to the insurance company and it's a wash. The twenty-five percent of my assets that Isabelle got, I'll split with her in a divorce.

"So I get nine percent of my money back from the kids and twelve and a half percent from Isabelle, and that's more than enough for me. I'll get a job. Hopefully something I like this time. I'd like to go back to publishing again, maybe as an editor. I don't need to be a CEO ever again. I don't want to." Philippe stared at him, fascinated. Everything he had said made perfect sense, had been carefully thought out, and was more than fair to all. He knew that Charlie's children would be thrilled by his return. He couldn't say the same for Isabelle. Like Charlie, he suspected she would prefer the money she had gotten to a live husband.

"You've gotten humble, my friend. But your 'widow' hasn't. She may not want to give anything up." Knowing Isabelle, Charlie realized that that was possible, and even likely. And she would put up a fight to keep it. He was prepared for that.

"Does she have a choice?"

"We can fight her on it. With you returning from the dead, she'll look pretty bad if she won't give you anything back, when you're giving her plenty of money and a damn fine château. She can always sell that if she wants money. She'll be losing the Jansen pension, half the money she got, and use of the apartment. But she'll still have a tidy sum, and the château is worth a great deal of money. As divorces go, she's making out like a bandit."

"I'm sure she preferred my being dead to a divorce, but that's the way it's shaking out." Charlie was still being more than generous with Isabelle, but he and Philippe both knew she wouldn't think so. Philippe knew she'd even been unhappy about what her own children had gotten. She wanted everything for her. "I doubt that she'll be happy to see me."

"How are you going to let her know you're here?"

"I'm not sure. Call her? You let her know? A text?"

"I don't think she'll consider it good news," Philippe said.

"I expect that. I want to take care of business with her and leave again for a while, and then I'll look for a job. She can move out of the apartment while I'm away."

Philippe wasn't exactly sure how, but he could tell that Charlie had changed. He seemed stronger and more sure of himself, more definite, less beaten down and defeated. He didn't seem downtrodden or depressed anymore. And then Philippe put his finger on it: Charlie seemed like a happy man. Philippe was glad for him. Charlie had been unhappy for a long time, enough so that he decided to walk out on his life, and stay gone for almost five months. It took guts to do that. And he'd been lucky enough to find a woman who suited him and made him happy. Philippe was relieved to hear he was leaving Isabelle. He had never liked her, she was greedy and hard.

"I think I should call her," Charlie said finally, pensive. He wasn't sure what to say, but they were still married, and he owed her an explanation. He fully recognized that what he had done was extreme.

Charlie and his lawyer spent two hours together, outlining how to proceed, and then he went to open a bank account, since all of his were closed, and get credit cards, so he could finally buy things without Aude's help. He called her after the meeting and told her how it had gone. And then he took a hotel room at the Four Seasons George V, which was not far from his lawyer. He was going to need Philippe's help for a while to sort things out and negotiate with Isabelle and her lawyer. He was going to call her first, and then his children.

He called Isabelle from his hotel room. She wouldn't have recognized the number of his new cell phone anyway. She answered cautiously, not sure who it was.

"Hi, Isabelle," he said in the most normal voice he could muster. "I have a lot to explain to you, but I'm back." There was silence at the other end for a full minute while she processed what he'd said and who it was. "I'm sorry. It must have been a hard five months," he said sympathetically.

"Are you serious?" she nearly shrieked into the phone. "You weren't dead and let everyone think you were? What kind of sick game was that? And now you're sorry and you want to come back?" She was shouting by then, in a total panic. She could imagine him taking back everything she had. And it was hers now if he was dead, which most inconveniently, he wasn't.

"I said I was sorry, not that I want to come back. I don't. It's way too late for us. It already was when I had the accident. We should have ended the charade years ago. I don't know why we didn't. Our marriage was much more dead than I ever was."

"So you did have an accident?" she asked him. "What happened? Have you had amnesia for all this time, or been in a coma?" It was the only way she could imagine his being silent for five months.

"I fell asleep at the wheel and drove off a cliff when I was driving up to the château after the meeting with Jerome. And by some insane miracle, I survived. I haven't been in a coma. I've been figuring out my life."

"What took you so long?" she said tartly. She was clearly not happy to hear from him, which wasn't a surprise.

"I had a lot to figure out. What went wrong with us. The job I hated and only kept so I could afford to keep you happy. We've been leading separate lives for years, which wasn't good for either of us. I don't know why we stayed together. Habit, I think.

We had no excuse after the kids left. Anyway, we have some business to take care of and then you'll be rid of me. I'm sorry if I made you unhappy. But at least you have the château."

"Are you taking that back?" She sounded panicked.

"Of course not. It was always meant to be yours. Now it is. We can work the rest out through our lawyers if you want. It might be easier that way." She didn't ask to see him, and he didn't want to see her either. Whatever she had felt for him was dead now. And she didn't say she was glad he was alive. She wasn't. And now that he was back, she was terrified of what "business" he wanted to conclude with her. She wanted everything she'd gotten in his will, but he was no longer dead, so that was going to be a problem. "I'm going to call the kids now. I want to tell them myself, if you don't mind."

"About the divorce?"

"No," he said softly, "that I'm alive. That seems more important for them to know first."

"Oh."

"I'll have Philippe call your lawyer to get things rolling. I think we both probably want to get this over with quickly." She didn't comment, and a minute later they both ended the call and hung up. He called Judith in New York. She shrieked when she heard her father's voice. He apologized for being gone for so long, told her about the accident, and promised to come to see her very soon. She was laughing and crying and telling him she loved him when she hung up. The money never even occurred to her. She was overjoyed that he was alive and he was back. She would gladly have given everything back just to have him alive.

He called Olivier next, and he cried too. They both did. They promised to talk at length when they saw each other, and Charlie promised to explain as best he could. But they had a lifetime to do that now. He didn't mention Aude to either of them. It wouldn't have been appropriate.

Isabelle had been on the phone with Stephanie the entire time, after she and Charlie hung up. She told Stephanie everything that had happened, and told her she was afraid Charlie would take it all back now, although he had already said the château was hers. But he was obviously going to want his money back now. He had to live on something. But so did she.

"You'll just have to fight him in the divorce," Stephanie said. She had experience with that. "Don't give up anything you don't have to," she advised her. "This is war. He probably has a girlfriend. Did you ask him?"

"No, he wouldn't tell me anyway. He sounds different. Stronger, something. He's not the same. I guess driving over a cliff is a wake-up call of some kind." And she had sounded different to him too. Harder, tougher, more entitled than ever.

"Just don't give anything up," Stephanie advised

her again. Judith called her mother after that, ecstatic over her father's call. And Olivier called her too, deeply moved to have his father back again. Neither of them seemed to be holding it against him that he had vanished for four and a half months and let them think he was dead. They were sure there was an explanation and gave him the benefit of the doubt. He had always been a reasonable person. Isabelle was annoyed by how forgiving they were prepared to be. They were just happy to know he was alive and loved them. Their values hadn't changed. Neither had hers.

Charlie had done everything he needed to for the moment, having spoken to his family and met with his lawyer. Philippe knew now what Charlie wanted to happen, and it was up to him to negotiate it. Charlie checked out of the room at the George V, and drove back to Normandy then to see Aude in her little beach cottage. He wanted to surprise her, and knocked on the door. Aude's face lit up the minute she saw him. He had only been gone for one night, and she had expected him to be gone for days or even weeks. He was planning to stay with her until his lawyer needed him in town again. He still wanted to call Jerome Jansen on the phone, and tell him the pension would be returned, even if Charlie had to pay it himself. He was the same honorable man he always had been.

The only bad news when Charlie saw Aude again was that she had called her ex-husband's caseworker at the prison, and the police hadn't found him yet. He was still on the run, but nowhere near her at least. Charlie was relieved to know she was safe in the cottage they had rented.

They spent the weekend exploring the area and had some excellent meals at nearby restaurants. He had returned with a wallet full of cash. Philippe had lent him an envelope full of money until his credit cards came through. He had all the money Aude had advanced him.

Charlie told her about the calls to his children, and thanked her for urging him to reach out to them. It had been the right thing to do. And in time, it would all fall into place. He could hardly wait to see them again, and for her to meet them.

And Aude noticed almost immediately that his wedding ring was gone. At last. She smiled broadly as soon as she saw it.

They spent a quiet weekend, walking on the beach, and she did sketches on the pad she'd brought with her. Neither of them liked knowing that Paul Pasquier was still on the run, but there was nothing they could do about it, and she was safe where they were now, in Équemauville.

*   *   *

On Monday, Charlie called Jerome and told him he was alive. He was shocked when Jerome started to cry on the phone. He admitted that when Charlie died it had been almost like losing a son, or a younger brother, which touched Charlie profoundly. Jerome was more human than he'd thought, and he'd considered Charlie a friend, whatever their differences. Jerome wasn't an evil person, he just had a different code of ethics from Charlie, and bad manners, and was unpleasant to work for. Charlie couldn't even remotely imagine working for him again or how he had for eleven years, no matter how good the money. He hadn't done it for Isabelle. But he couldn't do it anymore. It had nearly cost him his life.

Jerome asked Charlie to come back to work. They had replaced him, but Jerome wasn't happy with the new man and said he would fire him in an instant for Charlie.

"I'd let him go in a hot minute if you'll come back."

"I can't, Jerry," Charlie said, feigning regret. "I've been gone too long."

"Five months is nothing." Jerome offered him a raise and was impressed when Charlie told him he was going to return the pension. Charlie was a man of honor.

"What did you do about those stickers, by the way? The safety stickers you wanted to cancel and I insisted on, the night I had the accident."

Jerome tried to avoid answering for a minute and then he laughed. "I canceled them, of course." They both laughed at that. Jerome wasn't a bad man, just a stubborn old man, and he had been terrible to work for. There was nothing Jerry could do to induce him to come back, and he understood that by the end of the call. What he'd said about Charlie dying had touched Charlie's heart, and he knew it was heartfelt. Charlie liked Jerome better now that he was no longer his boss. He was a curmudgeon who only cared about money.

Charlie wanted to do something about a job too, and had put feelers out in publishing, but he had been away from the business for a long time. No one he called leapt at the chance to hire him again. He had been away from publishing for almost fourteen years.

"There's always Armand and the garage," he said to Aude when he told her about the calls.

"Something will turn up at the right time," she encouraged him, and believed it.

In the meantime, he wanted Aude to come to Paris with him, the next time he had to go. She felt shy about coming to the city and entering his world. She was more comfortable when he was in hers. She missed her cabin, but as long as her ex was at large, it wasn't safe to go back. Charlie was relieved knowing she was at the beach house, and Pasquier wouldn't find her there.

The day after he spoke to Jerome, Philippe

called Charlie to report on a conversation he'd had with Isabelle's attorney. The exchange had been tougher than he'd expected, and he said Isabelle was prepared to stand her ground. She had hired one of the most aggressive lawyers in Paris, and they had made veiled threats that she was considering accusing Charlie of feigning his own death to commit insurance fraud, and to shirk his responsibilities to her. It was an empty threat but she was using it as leverage on him.

"Considering how generous your will was, their threats are absurd and won't get them far. I contacted the insurance company after I met with you and told them you were planning to return the money, and they were impressed. We don't have a strong case for memory loss after the accident, since you were never admitted to a hospital, although you probably should have been after an experience like that. But we can certainly claim psychological trauma, which could easily have affected your judgment, and explain why it took you so long to make contact and come back. How reliable a witness do you think your artist friend would be? What kind of witness would she make?"

"Probably a very good one, she's a woman of integrity. But I'm not going to ask her to lie for me. The truth is I was fed up with my life, and miserable for years. I hated my job, and my boss, although he turns out to be a more decent guy than I thought. My marriage to Isabelle was down the tubes for even longer, enough so to consider letting myself drown when I was under the water. And then I guess my survival instincts kicked in, and I swam like hell to get out of the currents, up to the surface, and back on the rocks after the car went down. I clawed my way up the cliff face. But the last thing I wanted was to go back to a life I hated. I didn't want to ever come back. The only reason I did was to see my kids and not let them down. It took me four and a half months to force myself to come back.

"Nothing I'm asking her to return is unreasonable. She gets the château, I get the use of the Paris apartment, and the kids get to keep ownership, which is fair to them. I was never going to give her that apartment. I'm asking her to give back half the money and investments I left her, because I'm still alive and I need something to live on too, and I'm out of a job and don't know when I'll find one again. Maybe never.

"Fifty-three-year-old men are not in high demand if they're already out of the job market, which I am. I could go back to Jansen, but I'd rather cut my liver out with an ice pick. It was a miserable job for a company I never cared about. Working in plastics has never been my dream. If I had to, I'd rather take a lesser job back in publishing. I loved that world, and was stupid to leave it because I had a tantrum at thirty-nine. If I could get back in, I would, even at a lower salary. But so far no one is offering. I don't really want all the headaches that go with being CEO again.

"I don't see what Isabelle has to complain about. She gets to keep the château, and half my investment portfolio, which is more than she deserves and would get in an ordinary divorce."

"She wants the other half too," Philippe said somberly. "And I see exactly what her problem is. She hasn't found another rich husband yet, although I've heard rumors that she's working hard on it, thus far with no success. She's pretty transparent. She's after money, big money, yours or anyone else's. She's not particular on the subject. And the other problem is that very inconveniently, it turns out that you're not dead, so she has to give back the pension she got from Jerome Jansen. If you give her *all* your investments, and pay back Jerry Jansen yourself, so she gets to keep the pension, *and* the château, she'll be happy."

"And what do I get?" Charlie asked him.

"A giant pain in the ass for having married her in the first place, and nothing for you to live on. Oh, and she wants spousal support too, so you'd better be sure you get a big salary for your next job, because she wants most of that too. It's no wonder no one wants to marry her, she's a bloodsucker just waiting to draw blood. She can sell the château if she wants money that badly."

"She'll never do that. She loves it," Charlie said simply.

"Then I say we stick to our guns, and she gives back half your investments, and the pension, and you give her spousal support in proportion to your next salary. She can't expect more than that. You won't get out of spousal support because it's a long marriage. But she can't keep a pension for a man who isn't dead. No court will uphold that, and just because she collected it erroneously, as it turns out, she doesn't get to keep it. She's not being very elegant about this, although I'm not surprised. She grumbled about the will as soon as she got it, and how much the kids had gotten. She would have been perfectly happy to shortchange her own children. And she didn't want them using the apartment or visiting the château either." Charlie was surprised at that. "She's been giving lavish house parties there every weekend ever since you died . . . sorry, ever since June," Philippe corrected himself. "So let's stick with our position. While the investment portfolio is in dispute, we freeze it, and she can't touch even her half of it until it's resolved. How does that sound to you?"

"Fair and sensible. She'll come out of the marriage with a very expensive piece of real estate, and a very solid investment portfolio she can live on, and spousal support. That's the best I can do."

"It's better than most people would do." It was a demonstration of why Charlie'd been so unhappy married to her, because all she wanted was money from him. She didn't care about him. Isabelle had a cash register for a heart. "She's suggesting you take back more from the kids and give it to her," Philippe told him, outraged by her position, and her lack of generosity toward her own children. But it didn't surprise him or Charlie.

"I'm not going to do that," Charlie said quietly.

"That's what I told her attorney. I knew you wouldn't."

"We'll stand our ground and see what she does. I think they'll back down eventually," Philippe said calmly.

Charlie told Aude about it after they hung up. The contrast between the two women was stunning. One was gentle, kind, reasonable, nurturing, compassionate, and most of all loving. The other was as tough as nails and only cared about money. It was clear that she wasn't in the least happy that Charlie wasn't dead. Isabelle had become a hard person to love in her mature years, and Charlie didn't feel a shred of remorse for wanting to divorce her. Aude made no critical comments about Isabelle to him, but she understood better now why he wanted to walk out of his life and vanish. She wondered if Isabelle had always seen him as an opportunity, not a person, or if her feelings for him had dwindled to that over the years. Isabelle also wanted to be married to a man who was as rich and successful as her father, and while Charlie had been a success in business, he didn't have killer instincts. That was why the more gentlemanly field

of publishing appealed to him, and he had deep
emotional ties to it due to his parents, who had
both been writers, a novelist and a poet. He had
done well in publishing, and knew he would have
been smarter to stick with it. But he had been hot-
headed in his earlier years, and no longer was. He
had settled down to be mature and responsible,
and now he was more interested in the quality of
his life, and not sacrificing his principles for a buck.
It was one of the many reasons why Aude loved
him, and why they were well suited to each other.
Her philosophies were similar to his, and meshed
with his perfectly. They both wanted to work, but
at jobs they loved and that were meaningful to
them, and not to the exclusion of all else.

Philippe promised to stay in touch, and said he
was going to send a tough letter to Isabelle's lawyer, restating their position.

Charlie was agitated after the conversation, and
Aude calmed him. She suggested they go to a movie
that afternoon to distract him. And they went out
to dinner afterwards. When they went home, he
lay with an arm around her.

"I hope I didn't make a mistake coming back,"
he said quietly. "I don't want to spend the next two
years going to court against Isabelle. The marriage
is over, our kids are grown up. It seems like we
ought to just be able to let go."

"She doesn't want to let go of the money," Aude

summed it up. She realized now that there was real money involved, probably a lot of it.

"I just want to go back to your cabin," he said with a smile, "as soon as they send your ex-husband back to prison. Any news on that front?" he asked her.

"He's still on the run. They haven't caught him yet."

"At least I know you're safe here, if I have to go back to the city." The little cottage was a change of scene for them, with long beaches to walk on, and lots of good little restaurants around the town. Some of them were closed for the winter, but most were open. "I guess we knew things would be bumpy for a while when I went back. But at least the kids know I'm alive and I didn't abandon them." She had given him good advice, and the battle with Isabelle couldn't last forever. And hopefully, Aude's ex-husband would be back in jail soon, and they could lead a normal life. It was all he wanted now, and to share that life with Aude. It was all she wanted too.

Chapter 10

"Don't ease up on him for a minute. Sooner or later, he'll give up," Stephanie advised Isabelle. Isabelle didn't intend to give back a penny she didn't have to, and she had just met a man she liked at a dinner party. He had his own plane, and a boat. He was in his seventies, but Isabelle didn't care how old he was. He had a yacht and a jet. He had already promised to come to her next house party at the château.

He had invited her to go to his house in the Dominican Republic, where his boat was at the moment. He kept it in the Caribbean in winter, the Med in summer, and she was furious when her lawyer told her she couldn't go. She had to stay in town for a deposition, and that had to be her priority right now. She didn't tell Yves Napier, her new man, why she couldn't go. She said she had to deal with business issues relating to an investment. She didn't want him to know she was battling with her soon-to-be ex-husband over money. She thought it would make her seem greedy.

Charlie wasn't happy about it either. He had to go to Paris to be deposed too. He tried to get Aude to go with him, and attempted to lure her with revisiting the beauty of Paris. She hadn't been in years, and he wanted to share it with her. And she could visit her gallery. But she didn't want to interfere with his divorce. She had finally bought painting supplies, since they were stuck in Équemauville, and she wanted to get to work on a painting. She had loved Paris when she was younger, but she didn't want to go to the city with Charlie until the negotiation for the divorce was behind him. She was adamant about it. She didn't want to run into his wife.

She got up early with him the morning he left, made breakfast for him, wished him luck, and kissed him goodbye. As soon as he was gone, she got to work sketching on the canvas she wanted to paint. She was excited to be working again.

When she waved goodbye to Charlie, neither of them noticed the man watching them from his car across the street. He had a heavy black beard, was wearing a baseball cap pulled down low over his eyes, and was slouched down in his seat. He waited a few minutes, and then walked across the street toward the cottage. He used a remote control,

which opened the garage door soundlessly. It was a
generic control that would open almost any garage. Aude had parked her car on the street. The
garage was empty, and the door inside leading into
the house was unlocked. Within seconds, he was
standing in the kitchen facing her, the clicker back
in his pocket, and a hunting knife in his hand. She
jumped when she saw him standing only a few feet
from her. She didn't recognize his face with the big
black beard, but the moment he spoke, she knew
who he was, though she hadn't seen him in eight
years. It was Paul Pasquier, her ex-husband.

"Still painting?" he asked, as his eyes darted
around the room to make sure no one was there.
They were alone.

"What are you doing here?" she said, trying not
to show how frightened she was. His eyes shifted
constantly, and then bore into hers.

"I came to see you," he said with an evil smile
that peeked through his beard. "Just a little visit.
It's been a long time. Happy to see me?" She had a
palette knife on the table next to her, but it was no
match for his hunting knife, and she was no match
for him, and never had been. He was tall, with
broad shoulders and powerful arms. He'd been lift-
ing weights in prison and had gotten heavier.

"When did you get out of prison?" she said, con-
trolling her voice, and trying to figure out a fast
escape route, while she spoke to him. There was
none. He was between her and any door. He had

placed himself strategically. He was crazy, but also smart. This was the scenario she had always dreaded once he got out.

"I got out when I wanted to," he said cryptically. "A couple of weeks ago."

"You need to go," she said firmly, and he laughed.

"Why? Where's your boyfriend? And don't lie to me and tell me he's in the next room. I saw him leave. You go for the old ones now, huh?" Charlie was older than she was, but he wasn't old. Paul was thirty-eight, and he looked even crazier than before. His eyes burned like black fire. She wondered if he was on something, coke, speed, meth. He was hyped up, or maybe that was his natural state now. He seemed insane. He had been when he'd killed her lover.

"I want you to go," she said, raising her voice a notch, and he ignored her and walked around the kitchen, pacing.

"I'm not going anywhere. You're still painting," he said, glancing at the canvas.

"Paul, what do you want?" She tried to reason with him.

"You're my wife. I want you to act like one. Cook for me, clean my house, be a good wife, not lie and cheat on me, like you did. And now you're cheating on me again and being a whore."

"We're divorced," she said coldly, wondering how she'd ever get him out.

"You had no right to divorce me. Besides, it's not

legal. We're still married. You forgot to check some of the boxes."

"I checked all the boxes. We've been divorced for seven years." The conversation was pointless.

"You thought you could run away, like a coward. It was easy to find you on the internet, and your address was on the divorce papers. How did you like the pets I left you at the cabin?" He laughed at that. He was sick. His years in prison had rotted what was left of his brain. "Did you think you could get away from me by coming here? I followed you. You didn't even see me." She didn't answer his questions and accusations, and felt panic rise in a tidal wave. There was no escaping him. It was impossible to guess what he had in mind, and she was afraid he'd stay all day, waiting for Charlie to come back, and kill him too in a jealous rage, like the one that had landed him in prison. "I have a cabin too, you know. In the forest we used to go to. It hasn't changed. Maybe you'd like to see it again." She had gone there with him a few times when they were first dating. It was a beautiful place but too far to go, and too primitive. She had found it oppressive and too isolated. It had scared her. She had told Charlie about it once when they were talking about remote areas that weren't spoiled yet. Charlie liked places that were natural but more populated, with creature comforts. She and Paul had gone camping, with no electricity or plumbing, just unspoiled nature. It had been too rugged for her, but Paul loved it. He'd hunted a deer out of season. There was no one around to care or object, which he liked. Her last trip with him to that remote area had made her start to question the soundness of his mind.

When she'd met him, he was fun and exciting and a little wild, but didn't seem dangerous. And then later the jealousy had come out, the unfounded accusations for no reason, and long afterwards, his hatred of other humans. He had told her then about the abuse he'd suffered as a child, the punishments and beatings from his cruel parents. They had abandoned him eventually, and his foster parents weren't much better. His childhood and adolescence had ruined him. She had felt sorry for him, but not enough to stay. She had left him and started the affair with her school friend, Jean-Michel. She was planning to divorce Paul but hadn't yet. She couldn't afford to. What had started as carefree and exciting with Paul, who had a sexy daredevil side to him of unbridled youth, became terrifying, and ended in tragedy for her friend. It had marked her forever, and she felt guilty about Jean-Michel's death. She hadn't been with a man since, until Charlie. It had taken eight years for her soul to repair. And now Paul was back.

"Paul, there's nothing for you to do here. You should go now." She tried to sound calm and reason with him again.

"I'm not going anywhere. Make me something

to eat." She hesitated, not wanting to anger him, or to prolong his stay either, but he pulled her toward the refrigerator, and she thought maybe he'd leave if she fed him.

She made a sandwich with shaking hands and put it in front of him. He cut it in half with his hunting knife and ate it as though he was starving, and then he stood up, frighteningly near her, and reached into his pocket. For a second she thought he was going to pull out a gun and shoot her, but he brought his hand out with a fistful of cotton, or something that looked like it, in a plastic bag. He grabbed her by the back of her neck with one powerful hand, and covered her nose and mouth with the cotton. He'd stolen it, and the substance it contained, from the prison infirmary. It was ether.

She fought him, but the chloroform did its job quickly.

Her eyes rolled back in her head, and she went limp and dropped like a stone to the floor at his feet. He smiled when he saw her lying there and went to work instantly. He had come prepared. He had a roll of duct tape in another pocket, and used his hunting knife to cut a length of it and put it over her mouth. He bound her hands together behind her, and then her ankles. He ran to the bedroom and pulled a blanket off the bed, spread it on the floor, and rolled her into it. He left her there and went outside to drive his car into the garage and close the door again. Minutes later, he carried her into the garage and dumped her in the trunk of the small battered old car he had borrowed from a friend recently paroled out of prison. She was still unconscious. He opened the garage door with the remote and drove out again. Her cell phone was still on the kitchen table, and the lights were on, as it was a hazy day. The cottage looked cheerful and brightly lit as he drove away and headed north. He had a mission. This was just the beginning, but it had gone well so far. He turned on the radio as he drove, it was a perfect day for him. He had waited years for this moment. And now it had finally come.

The deposition of Charles Vincent was lengthy and thorough. He wasn't happy to be there, but answered the questions as his lawyer had directed. When he didn't remember something, he said so. Not remembering was acceptable. Lying obviously wasn't, and guessing was unproductive and not admissible.

Most of the questions were asking for precise details about his accident and how much he remembered afterwards, what he had done, his state of mind, why he hadn't called his wife or sought medical assistance. There were details about that night he sincerely didn't remember because he was injured, had suffered a blow to the head, and was in shock. Most of the decisions he had made that night and for several days afterwards were entirely understandable.

The next four months of silence from him, and hiding with determination, were harder to explain. But it was conceivable that the trauma and resulting PTSD were still a significant influence on him then. Isabelle's attorney informed Philippe that they would want a full psychiatric evaluation in order to determine if his actions were fraud-based or because he was psychiatrically impaired. But whatever Charlie's mental state after the accident, Philippe pointed out that his will had been written when he was of sound mind and expressed his wishes for the bequests to his heirs. Philippe objected to the line of questions and arguments since it was clear now that Charlie was not dead, and the will did not apply. Isabelle's lawyer tried to hold onto it as an argument, but finally gave up. He could always try again in court, if they got there because they couldn't agree to a divorce settlement.

The opposing lawyer asked Charlie if he had planned the accident, or had intended suicide. Charlie answered no to both questions. He was exhausted after a long day and had fallen asleep, and the road was dangerous. The lawyer asked why Charlie hadn't pulled over and taken a nap, and Charlie responded that he was trying not to disappoint his wife, since they had weekend guests, and he had promised to be there. And there was no shoulder on that stretch of road to pull over safely.

Isabelle's attorney asked him pointedly where he had been living in the months after the accident, and he told them. Then the lawyer asked if Charlie and Aude were lovers and he said they were. He asked if they had been lovers before the accident, or knew each other, and Charlie said he had just met her that night, having stumbled into her cabin after walking for several miles. Philippe was satisfied with his answers and thought Charlie conducted himself well. He didn't lose his temper, no matter how abrasive and accusatory the questioning was. He sounded honest, and was quiet and respectful to Isabelle's attorney, a junior lawyer he had brought with him, and Isabelle herself. She interrupted constantly, with comments, and her lawyer had to warn her to stop.

Her lawyer then asked Charlie a battery of questions about their spending habits, the lavish lifestyle to which Mrs. Vincent was accustomed, his job, his salary, his current employment plans, and his future ability to work after the accident. He asked Charlie how he had supported himself for nearly five months after the accident, since there had been no activity whatsoever on any of his bank accounts or credit cards. Charlie stated simply that he had taken a job as a car mechanic in a local garage. He stunned Isabelle and her lawyers with that, and Philippe enjoyed it so much, he laughed,

and then apologized. Isabelle looked outraged. Her
lawyer asked Charlie if he had intended to come
back eventually, and Charlie said he wasn't sure.
He thought so, to see his children, but he hadn't
decided until he actually took action and did it. He
also answered that Aude had loaned him money
when he had none, and when asked how much, he
said it was four hundred and twenty-nine euros,
and that he had paid her back.

Everything that came out of the deposition
made him look and sound like an honest man, with
integrity, who had been through a shocking experience, and had been confused for several months
about what to do next. None of it had been pre-
meditated, intentionally fraudulent, or intended to
harm his wife.

The deposition took four hours. Charlie was exhausted afterwards and looked it. They broke for
lunch, and Philippe was going to depose Isabelle
afterwards, which he expected to be interesting,
particularly on financial matters.

Charlie called Aude on her cell phone as soon as
it was over, before lunch, and she didn't answer. He
thought she might have gone for a walk, or was
concentrating on her painting and might have si-
lenced the phone so she didn't get interrupted. He
was disappointed not to talk to her, but not worried. He and Philippe had lunch at Philippe's office
to go over the questions for Isabelle again, and they
arrived back in the conference room promptly at

two-thirty. Isabelle was twenty minutes late, and no one commented when she showed up.

The questions for Isabelle had been carefully prepared, to give as precise an idea as possible to the vast amount of money she spent frivolously and to indulge herself, for her house parties, for decorating the château and their apartment, and for her wardrobe. What Philippe was able to show was a woman who was extravagant, a spendthrift, and vastly self-indulgent at her husband's expense, and what enormous pressure it put on Charlie to earn in order to keep up. She thought she was justifying the amount she wanted in spousal support, but in fact, it actually made her look worse and less deserving. She had wasted a fortune for years, for expenditures that weren't justifiable, or even reasonable, and no judge would sympathize with her.

Philippe interrupted the financial questions at one point to surprise her with some unexpected questions about how soon she had started dating after Charlie's disappearance. She answered primly that she didn't remember. She also didn't remember who or how many men she had dated. He asked her for a rough estimate, and she finally glared at the lawyer and said twenty, or maybe twenty-five. He looked startled by the answer, and estimated it to be four or five a month, and acted as though he thought it was a lot. Charlie had to strain to keep a straight face. She'd been busy in his absence and had started auditions early. She claimed not to remember who the men were and volunteered no names, but Charlie was sure they were all wealthy men. They would have to be to pass muster with her and meet her needs in future if Charlie's money ran out.

If nothing else, how unsuited they were to each other was abundantly clear after the depositions. Isabelle gave Philippe a long verbal list of the kinds of things she needed her spousal support for, and the amounts and items themselves were shocking. She wanted to live like a princess forever, at Charlie's expense. But the gravy train was leaving the station, especially if he took a lesser job, which he said he might. He wasn't going to take another soul-crushing job he hated, with adult children who were employed now, in order to support his ex-wife, while he lived more simply himself to facilitate her much more extravagant lifestyle. She could no longer expect that of him, which had her panicked unless she found a new husband soon, with a lot more money. The man she was currently dating, Yves Napier, whose name she did remember, sounded like a viable candidate, with a yacht, a private plane, and several houses.

During every break in the proceedings, Charlie had called Aude at the cottage again and she didn't answer. Since he hadn't talked to her all day, and the depositions ended at seven P.M., he decided not to spend the night at the hotel after all. He'd booked a room at the Crillon this time, but he canceled it and drove back to see her. He wanted to tell her about the depositions, and to be with her for comfort's sake. It had been stressful listening to Isabelle's answers to Philippe's questions all day, and he missed Aude. They were used to spending so much time together now that a day apart seemed like a lifetime, and she always had such an intelligent perspective on things. He was eager to hear her thoughts now.

Charlie ran the questions and responses over in his mind on the way to the little summer beach town where they were staying. There was traffic on the road, and after his debriefing session with his lawyer to analyze the proceedings, it was nine o'clock when he pulled up in front of the cottage. It was brightly lit and looked cheerful, and he smiled thinking of Aude waiting for him. He couldn't wait to see her. She hadn't answered his calls all day, nor returned them.

He hurried up the steps, let himself in with his key, and called out to her. She wasn't in the kitchen or the bedroom, he could tell as he walked in, and when he walked into the kitchen, he saw a plate on the table, heard the radio playing, and noticed a kitchen chair was overturned. Her cell phone was on the table with all his messages listed. She hadn't read any of them. He could feel panic rise in his throat. He ran into the bedroom to check again and saw that the blanket had disappeared, and the bedspread was dumped on the floor, which wasn't like her. There was a feeling in the house as though she had left to go somewhere in haste, but when he glanced outside, he saw that her car was there, so she hadn't gone out. She could have gone for a walk, but he didn't have that impression. He noticed then that the inside door to the garage was open, and he wondered for an instant if someone had gained access to the house through the garage. He and Aude didn't keep that door locked. He thought they should but Aude kept forgetting.

Charlie wanted to cry as he looked around and couldn't find her, and when he looked down at the kitchen floor, he saw a length of roughly cut duct tape stuck to it, and he was terrified about what might have happened. He could sense in his gut that someone had been there and something terrible had occurred. Aude was gone. And he knew instantly that she'd been taken, and that Paul Pasquier had found her and taken her.

Chapter 11

Driving straight north, without stopping anywhere, keeping up his speed even on the hairpin turns later in the trip, and with less traffic early in the day, it took Paul just over an hour to get to the cabin Aude and Charlie had left only days before, to escape him. There was no one around, and the house was well hidden from the main road, so he had no need to hide what he was doing. He opened the trunk, pulled the blanket off Aude's face, and looked at her. She was awake but still groggy, and seemed confused when she saw him. She couldn't speak with the tape over her mouth. Her wrists were tightly bound and her shoulders yanked back, her legs pulled up and her ankles attached to each other. Her long blond hair was tangled, and as she regained consciousness in the fresh air once the trunk was open, she looked frightened.

"Have a nice ride?" he asked her. His hunting knife hung from his belt in a new leather sheath. He had bought it as soon as he left prison, along with the other supplies he knew he'd need. He could kill a man with a knife if he had to, and he had an automatic rifle under a tarp on the floor of the backseat. A prison buddy on parole had loaned him the car once he escaped. He had promised to return it. The plan had been prearranged before his friend left prison months earlier. Paul had already been planning his escape then.

Paul sold drugs to the other prisoners while he was still inside, to save up the money he'd need once he was out. He had planned his escape carefully, and so far nothing had gone awry. He knew that the police would be looking for him, but he was staying well below the radar and avoiding anyplace with crowds or police. Now that he had Aude in his possession, he could disappear so no one could find them. He owed her eight years of pain for the divorce. In his mind, it was her fault he'd gone to prison, for being a whore, having a boyfriend once they separated and sleeping with him, so Paul had had no choice but to kill him. He had a score to settle now with the new guy too. In his mind, their blood was on her hands, not his. He was only doing what any man would do. There was no question in his mind that she was to blame, and had to pay for the crimes she had committed against him.

He picked her up out of the trunk, threw her over his shoulder like a sack of grain, kicked the door to her cabin open with a heavy boot, walked in, and dumped her on the living room floor. With one glance, she knew where she was. She was home, in her cabin, under the worst conditions imaginable, as his prisoner. Her eyes followed him everywhere. He looked in the refrigerator and kicked it hard when he found it empty. She and Charlie had left no food there, since they didn't know when they'd come back. The cupboards were almost bare too. Paul took out some cereal, filled a bowl with it and added water, and ate it as he watched her.

"Nice place you have here," he said ironically, as she lay on the floor and watched him, fearful of what he'd do next. He was in no hurry now. He knew that no one would find them there, not for a while at least, and by then they'd be gone. He could live for months in the forest, eating what he hunted and killed.

He glanced at her paintings neatly arranged in the kitchen and shrugged. He looked into cupboards, opened drawers, and found nothing of interest. He dumped the contents on the floor as Aude lay on the floor and watched him take her home apart. They stayed for an hour, and she wondered if he was going to keep her hostage there. If so, Charlie would come to look for her, and she was sure that Paul would kill him. She wondered if he was going to kill her first. His bloodlust was in his eyes. He had brought his rifle in from the car in case he needed it. He was still dumping things on the floor while she watched him, his rifle leaning in a corner near the door. She hoped they would stay the night and give Charlie and the police time to find them. She couldn't say a word with the tape on her face. Paul rambled to himself and to her as he searched the entire cabin, and then went out to the car to get something. He came back with two heavy cans of gasoline and set them down near her.

He opened the cans and started splashing the gasoline everywhere as she watched with wide, frightened eyes. It was obvious what he was going to do with the gas, but she had the distinct impression he was going to set fire to her too.

He guessed what she was thinking and shook his head. "That would be too easy. You have a job to do, you're coming with me to be my wife. And you're not going to need this place anymore, so I thought we'd kiss it goodbye. There's nothing here you'll need where I'm taking you." Everything she loved and had gathered for the past eight years was in that cabin, along with a few mementos of her parents. It was the only home she had, and it had been a haven of safety and peace for her for all eight years. Now he was defiling it and was going to destroy it. He opened several of the books and set the pages on fire, dropped them on the floor, and lit the curtains, while she lay silent and bound and watched him. With the gas splashed everywhere, the fires caught quickly, and within minutes the cabin and its contents were ablaze.

He had left her on the floor while he did it, and just when she was sure her hair would catch fire, or her clothes, he picked her up, threw her over his shoulder again, walked out to the car, dumped her in the trunk, and closed it. He took a last look at the cabin and smiled, and then got in the car, put it in gear, and bumped down the dirt road that led to Aude's home. The whole cabin was burning by then. It was time to leave. Someone would see the smoke eventually, but there would be nothing left of it. He had doused her paintings generously, particularly the portrait of a man who looked like her boyfriend. She would have nothing to come back to after this, and no one in her life but him, which was what he wanted.

She had caused him untold pain with years of prison and now she was going to pay for it. If her boyfriend showed up somewhere, Paul would kill him too, and it would be her fault if he did. But where he was going, he was sure no one would find them. He had no intention of going back to prison. They were going to live by his wits from now on. He owned her now. She would never escape him again.

He stopped to buy food along the way, and after

that at a pawnshop and pawned her watch. He kept his baseball cap on, pulled down low. Aude hadn't had food or water all day, but he didn't want to take the tape off until they got to the cabin where he was taking her. He'd never even seen a forest ranger there. No humans. They would be the only ones. It was a long drive, but they could spend years there without being discovered, and the wildlife was plentiful for a hunter. He would have her cook it for him. In the meantime, she could do without food and water until they got there. It wouldn't kill her. Only he would do that, if she didn't do as she was told. Even if she tried to escape, he'd find her. He knew the forest, and how to survive in it. She didn't.

Paul Pasquier had been driving for several hours when Charlie arrived at the beach house and found Aude gone. He went to the police station to report her missing, and said he thought she'd been kidnapped. They were skeptical until he told them that her ex-husband was an escaped convict currently on the run, which piqued their interest. They checked their computers and found the report and Paul Pasquier's details. There was currently a search on for him, and they told Charlie that police in the entire region were looking for him. He tried to explain to them that Pasquier had Aude with him as a captive now, he was sure of it. They added the information to the computer, to be read by anyone checking for Paul Pasquier. Charlie gave them a description of Aude, and she was added to the bulletin about Pasquier, but the police told him that for now, there was nothing they could do. They would question the neighbors in the morning, to find out if they'd seen anything, but they had nothing else to go on. No description of a vehicle, no eyewitnesses, no license plate, no clear evidence left at the scene. It was all guesswork on Charlie's part, and might not even be true. She was gone from the rented cottage, but Charlie had found no hard evidence of Paul Pasquier.

Charlie went back to the cottage, and then wondered if Paul might have taken her back to her cabin. It was a long shot, but he decided to drive there and see.

It gave him a little shiver when he drove past the spot on the road where he'd fallen months before, and he arrived at the cabin in the dark of night. But even in the dark, he could see what had happened. Her cabin had burned to the ground, the embers still smoldering and the fire sizzling. The cabin was gone, and everything in it reduced to ash, even her paintings. He could see the gas cans under the rubble, and knew even without seeing them that it was arson, and who had done it. But there was no sign of Aude anywhere. Charlie was terrified that Paul might have left her to burn in the fire. He called the police immediately to report it.

They were there twenty minutes later, with the fire department and an ambulance. The firefighters searched the rubble and found no human remains, so she wasn't dead in the fire, but it confirmed to Charlie that Paul had taken her hostage and had taken her with him. He told the police that he believed that Pasquier was holding her captive, although he couldn't prove it. They believed him, and were sympathetic and concerned. There was no hard evidence, just guesses and supposition based on her disappearance and Paul's history. Charlie gave them his cell phone number and they promised to call if there was any news, or if Aude was seen somewhere with Pasquier. He was listed as extremely dangerous and armed, and the police assured Charlie that the search for Paul Pasquier was of the highest priority to them, and he hoped it was true.

He slept in his car in the village for a few hours after that. He had nowhere else to go, and it was too late to get a hotel room or a bed-and-breakfast. He was waiting outside the garage when Armand arrived in the morning. He was surprised to see Charlie standing there, looking grim.

"What happened?" Armand unlocked the front doors and made Charlie a cup of coffee while he told him about Paul still being on the run and Aude's disappearance the day before, that he was convinced her ex-husband had her with him, and that the police had a nationwide search on for both Pasquier and Aude.

"They'll never find him," Armand said, sipping the steaming coffee that Charlie missed sharing with him almost every day.

"Why not?" Charlie looked crestfallen when he said it. Armand seemed convinced.

"They don't have the manpower. The country is threatened with terrorist attacks every day. There's dangerous stuff happening in the cities. And your man is free to roam all over the country. They're even more short-staffed in rural areas like this, and it sounds like that's what this guy knows best. He can hide for years. You have to find her," Armand said seriously. "There's no telling what the guy will do to her. He sounds insane. He's already murdered two men. He'll do it again, or a woman."

"That's what I'm trying to do, find her," Charlie said, desperate. He looked rough after the night before.

"You should hire a private detective, not count on the police in their limited free time while they're trying to deal with a hundred problems at once. I have the feeling you can afford it. It will be money well spent. Hire someone good who can outsmart him, and find our girl," Armand said somberly, "before he kills her." His words sent chills up and down Charlie's spine, and made it seem even more urgent.

Charlie called Philippe Delacroix from his cell phone while still at the garage. "I need a private detective," Charlie said in a tense voice as soon as Philippe came on the line.

"It won't do you any good," Philippe said, unenthused.

"Why not?" Charlie was discouraged the minute he heard it.

"Because a judge isn't going to care how many rich men Isabelle sleeps with in order to find her next meal ticket. People don't care about that anymore. It's all about mathematics now, and what percentage of your money a judge thinks she should get for thirty years of marriage." Charlie almost laughed except that he was in no mood to do so.

"I don't give a rat's ass who Isabelle sleeps with. I could care less. This is something much more important. The woman I've been living with disappeared last night. She has a criminal ex-husband, who was in prison for murder but escaped a few weeks ago. There was some evidence that he might have been watching her, so we moved to a temporary location a few days ago. She vanished yesterday while I was at the deposition. And someone burned her cabin to the ground last night, with gas cans all over the place. The police have it all in their computers, but they're understaffed and not doing much about it. I'm afraid he'll kill her. She divorced him when he went to prison, and he's not happy about it."

"Oh my God, that's awful. I know a good guy. He's an ex-cop, and an army-trained commando. He does missing persons, deals with industrial espionage, and a lot of heavy-duty stuff. I'll look him up and text you his details. Keep me posted."

Less than a minute later, Charlie had the desired information by text message. The detective's name was Robert Bercy, and Philippe had sent his email address and cell phone number. Charlie was still at Armand's garage when he called him. Bercy answered immediately and sounded busy. He was businesslike and to the point, and Charlie explained the situation to him.

"Where do you think he is now?"

"I have no idea. The cabin I think he burned to the ground is more than two hours outside Paris, depending on traffic, in Normandy. I have no idea where he'd go from here. Probably somewhere secluded where no one will see them. He's kind of a mountain man type, hunts, fishes, likes to live off the land, hates people, likes to shoot a rifle or kill an animal when he feels like it, and if he has her with him now, he'll have to be extra careful no one sees her."

"Let me do a computer search of the area and see what kind of dense forestry we have in the vicinity or on a straight line from there. He probably has her concealed somewhere in his car, so he won't want people looking in and checking on him." The thought of Aude tied up and hostage to a man like Pasquier made Charlie feel sick.

"I think we have to find him fast before he kills her."

"I get that. I know the type," Bercy said.

"How do the police feel about your getting involved? Will it make them back off or be less interested?" Charlie was worried about that too, and he didn't want to rely entirely on a complete stranger, even if Philippe said he was good. And he didn't want the police to get their noses out of joint and stop looking for Pasquier.

"I work with them all the time. I'm very collaborative. I won't step on their toes, but I have more time on my hands to pursue it. They have a lot of big problems these days, bigger than one escaped convict, even though there could be a life at stake here, and time is crucial." It was exactly what Charlie wanted to hear, was willing to pay for, and able to afford. "I'll call you back," Robert Bercy promised, and Charlie went to tell Armand that he had followed up on his suggestion and had hired a detective.

"You work fast," Armand said to him.

"It was a good idea, and I love her," Charlie said simply, and went to sit on a stool in the garage while Armand got to work. He didn't ask Charlie to help him. Charlie had more important things to do. Bercy called him back half an hour later.

"There are three distinct areas that came up in

my search. It takes two days to get to one of them, and it's too hard to access. The two others are distinct possibilities. I'm not sure which to consider first. One of them is more rugged. There isn't a human around, or a house. It's incredibly rustic and primitive, no plumbing or electricity, no population. The other is slightly more civilized, it's a twenty-six-thousand-acre national forest with a few houses or cabins here and there, but not many, and a campground that's only used in summer."

"I think the second one, from the way you describe it . . . what's it called?"

"La Forêt de Tronçais," Bercy told him, and an electric current went through Charlie.

"Oh my God. She told me about it, she went there with him a couple of times and hated it. I think that's where he's going. It makes sense."

"It's about a five- or six-hour drive from where you are, in the Massif Central. It's twenty-six thousand acres of thick underbrush and heavy forest. It's almost impassable except on foot or by mule. There are a few tracks where you can get a car in, but not many. I'll warn the police in the area now, and I can pick you up late this afternoon, and drive up with you. We won't get there till midnight, but we'll be there at first light to start looking. Bring a sleeping bag, we can sleep in my SUV."

Charlie thought of something else then. "Are you armed?"

"Yes," Bercy said without hesitating. "Legally so.

I'm an ex-cop. Only active cops, retired police, licensed hunters, and the military can bear arms in France," he reminded him, which Charlie knew. He was relieved to hear that Bercy was armed. They might need a gun. "Where shall I pick you up?" Charlie gave him the address of Armand's garage, and Bercy said he'd be there by six, possibly earlier if he could. Charlie asked him briefly about the cost of hiring him, just so he knew. He would have paid any amount to find her. Bercy gave Charlie a ballpark figure for his daily rate, depending on the circumstances, and Charlie approved it.

He went to tell Armand about the conversation and the plan then, and as he did, he grabbed a pair of overalls from a hook.

"You want to work today?" Armand asked him in surprise.

"If I don't do something to keep busy, I'll go nuts worrying about her."

"There's a set of brakes that need checking over there." Armand pointed to a car in a corner of the garage, and Charlie grabbed a tool kit and headed toward it. Then he remembered something.

"Do you have a sleeping bag I can borrow?" he called out to Armand.

"Yes, at home. I'll pick it up at lunchtime." Charlie waved his thanks and headed toward the car that needed a brake check. It was something to do so he didn't lose his mind, worrying about Aude.

Charlie called Paul Pasquier's caseworker that

morning too, and reported that there was a strong possibility that Pasquier had kidnapped his ex-wife and was now traveling with her. Charlie reported that her cabin had mysteriously burned to the ground the night before, the work of an arsonist. Virgil Thomas promised to get it on the nationwide computers and asked him for a photograph of Aude, which Charlie sent him a few minutes later. The police had taken a copy of it too.

Charlie worked on a truck and several cars most of the day. By five-thirty, he was wearing a down jacket, jeans, a heavy sweater, and a pair of hiking boots he had bought that afternoon. He had a small bag of toiletries, and Armand's sleeping bag under his arm. He looked tense and nervous. Robert Bercy showed up promptly at six, tall and powerfully built, somewhere in his late forties, with military bearing. He had been a commando in the military until a few years before when he had opened his protection and security business, and he had been a police officer before that. He looked like a good man to rely on, and Armand wished them luck when they left. Charlie was trying not to think what might be happening to Aude by then, if she was still alive. All they could do was what they were doing, everything possible to find her, get her away from her ex-husband, and bring her home.

Armand waved as they drove away, and Charlie couldn't see that there were tears in his friend's eyes. Armand just hoped they were in time to save her, if everything Charlie said about her ex-husband was true, and he believed him.

Chapter 12

By the time they got to the edge of the forest where Paul was planning to take her, Aude was in a daze in the trunk of the car, dozing. She had gone from panic to despair to hope that she could escape once they stopped. And finally, having eaten nothing all day and had nothing to drink, she felt like she was in a fog. She had wet her jeans hours before for lack of a bathroom stop and didn't care. She had watched him burn down her home, and everything she loved, and she knew what he was capable of. She knew that if she stayed, he would kill her. Her only hope of survival was to find a way to escape whenever she could, and she would have to do everything possible to find a way out of wherever he was taking her.

They had traveled a long way, and she had no idea where she was. She wondered if they had crossed the border into another country, but she thought it more likely that he was looking for some remote region where no one would see them. She didn't know what Charlie would do when he found her gone, and she didn't want him to fall into Paul's trap and become his victim too.

She woke up with a start when the car stopped and didn't move for a long time. It was hot and stuffy in the trunk, and her jeans had dried by then. She didn't know for exactly how long, but they had been on the road for many hours. He left her in the trunk for a while after they stopped. She wondered if they were going to drive on, or had reached their destination.

It was dark when he opened the trunk, grabbed her roughly, and pulled her out. She was so stiff she couldn't stand up by then. She stumbled and leaned against the car while he pulled the tape off her ankles, took her shoes, and put them in the deep pockets of his hunting jacket.

"There are jagged rocks here, pinecones, broken branches, and if you try to run, your feet will be cut to shreds and you won't get far. And wherever you go, I'll find you," he said harshly. She couldn't respond with the tape on her mouth, and he didn't remove it from her wrists either. He only freed her ankles so she could walk and he didn't have to carry her. She would have to manage with her hands taped behind her back. If she tripped or fell, she couldn't stop herself and would fall face-first.

"When I trust you, I'll take the tape off. You'll have to prove to me you're a good wife before I do," he said, and she saw the mad gleam in his eyes, had to fight waves of panic, and didn't react.

She could see that they were in a forest. The moon was shining overhead, but the foliage was heavy and the trees tall. She had the feeling she'd been there before, and wondered if it was the place that was so primitive she had hated it. She couldn't tell in the dark. They could have been anywhere, even another country, bordering France. There was no way to know. He took a heavy backpack with his supplies out of the backseat and left her standing there for a minute while her eyes adjusted. The night air was cold, and she was shivering when he came back to where she was standing and slapped her as hard as he could across the face. She was stunned when he hit her and hadn't expected it. She had done nothing to anger him. The force of the blow knocked her to the ground, and she didn't get up for a minute. She could feel a trickle of blood run down her cheek, as she lay on the ground with her eyes full of tears.

"There's lots more where that came from, so re-member it," he said viciously. "Any time you don't do as you're told, or piss me off, that's what you'll get. You get fed if you behave, and if you don't, I don't care if you starve. The food I brought is for me. You get fed when I want to feed you, if you deserve it. Get up. We have to walk in from here," he said, and left her to follow him barefoot, with her arms taped behind her back, so her balance was off, and the ground was as harsh on her feet as he had said. He wore the heavy backpack and carried a small bag. He left the rest of his things in the car to carry in later. There was no one here to take anything, or disturb them, or see them. Aude had the feeling that they could live there for years and never see a human.

She stumbled many times, fell on her knees hard once on a tree root, and followed him as best she could. They wove their way through the forest, and he seemed at home there. She noticed then that he had his high-powered rifle slung over his shoulder. She had the feeling that they were at the end of the world. There was nowhere to run to, and no way to escape. She would be there with him for as long as he wanted her to be, maybe years. She remembered reading about stories like that in the newspapers, as tears ran down her cheeks.

They passed a river and a small ravine, and after they had walked for a long time, she saw a small cabin, more like a hut, with a shed next to it and what appeared to be an outhouse behind it. She remembered it now. It was the place he had brought her twice after she married him, a place that she had hated. That was the first time she had suspected he was mentally deranged. He had killed a fawn and its mother, and laughed. He had acted strangely the whole time they were there. He had seemed more normal, or pretended to be, when they went back to civilization. She had had a miserable time in this place. It was the same hut they had stayed in before.

He dropped his heavy pack on the floor of the hut, and a sleeping bag, and stood in the doorway to block her from entering when she caught up to him. She could hardly walk on the cuts on her feet. He fumbled in his backpack, took out some tools, a padlock, and a chain, and pushed her toward the shed next to the hut where he left his things.

"Come on." He opened the door of the shed. There was some animal excrement in it. He nailed a steel ring to the wall, ran the heavy chain through the ring, and then wrapped the chain around her waist several times and put the padlock on it. It was a rudimentary way of attaching her to the wall of the shed so she couldn't escape. She could just manage to sit down with it, and almost lie down but not quite. She'd have to sleep leaning against the wall, but she no longer cared. Before he closed the padlock, he removed the chain, grabbed her roughly by the arm, and dragged her toward the outhouse. She stepped on a nail sticking out of a board. He took the tape off her wrists and shoved her into the outhouse, waited for her to come out, and taped her wrists again when she did. He wasn't taking any chances. He dragged her back into the shed then, put the padlock back on, and left her with the door open so he could hear her, and see her if he looked out the window of his hut. But she was wide open for any animal to attack her with no way to defend herself. The most dangerous animal in the forest was Paul.

"Don't worry. If anything comes after you, I'll shoot it," he shouted. And if he missed, he'd shoot her. She couldn't understand how anyone could treat another human the way he did. With every passing moment she could see the evidence of how sick and twisted he was, and how full of fear and hatred. There was no peace for him anywhere. He was a thousand times sicker than when she'd met him years before. They'd only stayed married for a very short time. He had become increasingly violent and dangerous in a matter of months, as though everything in him was mis-wired and defective. Now there was only hate and madness left, and punishment to be meted out. He was cruel to a frightening degree.

She sat chained to the wall, with the tape still over her mouth, and thought about her fate until she fell asleep. She woke at sunrise, but couldn't go anywhere. She just sat there, thinking of how she would escape one day, maybe when he trusted her more and gave her a little more freedom. There had to be a way. She couldn't give up hope.

He showed up an hour or two later, used the outhouse himself, and then unchained her and shoved her into it, and afterwards taped her up and chained her to the wall again, without speaking to her. Before he left her again, he ripped the tape off her mouth with no warning and took some skin with it. She could taste the blood on her lips. He handed her a bottle of water to drink from, and she choked as she guzzled it. She'd had no food or water since he'd kidnapped her. It was all punishment for divorcing him and, in his view, cheating on him, once they were separated. He was the distributor and designer of all punishments. "You can scream all you want," he told her. "There's no one to hear you anyway." She didn't make a sound. There was no point, and she didn't want to anger him and have him hit her again.

She knew where she was now. It was a national forest where he had taken her before. She remembered that there were eagles in the tall trees and he had shot one of them, which was illegal at any time of year. It was a nature preserve, which didn't matter to him either. He had as little respect for animals as he did for humans. Doing anything he wasn't supposed to gave him a thrill, particularly if there was death involved.

He disappeared for a long time that morning, and she heard gunshots. He came back empty-handed with his rifle, pointed it at her for an instant just to frighten her, then laughed and went back into his hut for something to eat. She hadn't eaten in more than twenty-four hours by then. He came back and threw two granola bars at her, leaving her hands untaped long enough to eat them and drink another bottle of water. Then he taped her up again with fresh tape, even tighter than before. The tape was cutting her wrists, and her hands were numb. He went back to his car for more supplies then, and carried in two bags of groceries. She remembered from before that they'd bought food from a grocery store a long way away. It had taken them half an hour to get there. He put a bottle of milk at the edge of the stream to keep it cool, since they had no refrigeration, and he would have to cook over a campfire he hadn't bothered to build yet, but he would. When he shot something he wanted to cook, he'd build a fire. He seemed completely at home in the woods.

Robert Bercy and Charlie reached the same forest from a slightly different angle shortly after midnight the same night that Paul and Aude had arrived. They had no way of knowing if the others were there too. The forest was huge and its perimeters confusing. They slept in the SUV and, in the morning, walked around looking for signs of humans and found none. Paul's car was well hidden behind some bushes. Robert and Charlie heard gunshots in the morning, so they knew someone was there, but they never saw anyone. There was no way of knowing if the shooter was Pasquier, and they weren't even sure if he was there with Aude.

Robert and Charlie had concealed the SUV, so no one would find evidence of their presence.

"You could be in this forest for months, and still be lost," Robert said to Charlie. "It's an eerie place. I've been here once before and it gave me the creeps."

"It's giving me the creeps now," Charlie admitted. "Where do you think they are?"

"In there somewhere, if they're here," Robert said, pointing to the heart of the forest. The gunfire they'd heard gave Charlie hope they were, and the shots hadn't seemed far away. It comforted him to think that Aude might be somewhere nearby, even if they didn't know where yet. They had to find her, and he prayed she was still alive.

Paul threw Aude a slice of ham and an apple for lunch, and a canteen of water, and before he freed her hands, he slapped her hard across the face again, and kicked her in the stomach with his hiking boot.

"For every moment of pain you've given me, that's what you get," he said to her, and then untaped her hands so she could eat. She no longer wanted to. The kick had given her a stomachache. She was grateful that he seemed to have no sexual interest in her. His only interest in her was punitive. All he wanted to do was kick and punch and hurt her. He gave her just enough food to keep her alive, but never a real meal, and she could only drink when he freed her hands and handed her a small bottle to drink from, so she was starving and dehydrated all the time. It made her dizzy, but so did the blows.

He shot some birds that afternoon and cooked them for his dinner after he cleaned them, but didn't offer her any. She got another granola bar instead. She wondered when he might run out of food and have to go to the store to stock up again. That might be her chance to escape, if she could find a way out of her chains. They looked worthy of Houdini, the way he had her chained up. He hadn't bothered to tape her mouth again. Her lips were scabbed and cracked.

"You've said yourself there's nowhere for me to go, and I can't walk on all the broken branches and pinecones and thorns in bare feet, so why do I have to be chained up all the time?" she asked him, once he stopped taping her mouth. He didn't bother to answer, but he left her unchained for longer after that and let her go to the outhouse alone. There was nowhere for her to turn to.

Robert and Charlie heard the shots when Paul killed the birds for his dinner, so they knew he and Aude weren't far, if it was them, but they couldn't see them at all in the dense forest. There was no sign of human life there at all other than occasional gunfire.

Bercy used a pair of long-distance infrared binoculars that night, and saw nothing at first, and then stopped moving them, and stayed focused on one spot.

"There's a campfire about half a mile away, straight through those trees," he whispered. "It's got to be them. There's no one else here." He didn't need to whisper but the fire seemed so close in his lenses.

"Can you see either of them?" Charlie whispered too.

"Just the flames of the fire." Then Robert saw a powerfully built male with a baseball cap turned away from them. He had no doubt. It was Paul Pasquier. "I've got him," he whispered to Charlie. "There's no sign of her. He may have her locked up, or chained to a tree." She might also be dead, but he didn't say it to Charlie. He was worried enough. Bercy continued to watch but didn't see the man again, and at midnight, he and Charlie went back to his car and contacted the police to tell them they'd seen Pasquier and where they were. The police wanted further confirmation before they sent SWAT teams in. Robert and Charlie promised to report to the police the next day.

* * *

The next day, their third in the forest, Aude was surprised when Paul didn't put the tape back on her wrists after her morning trip to the outhouse. Bercy had been intently watching the location of the flames he'd seen the night before, assuming it was their campsite. He saw no one until that night, when he caught glimpses of Paul several times in the same location, but never Aude. Paul seemed to go in and out of a shed next to the main hut, as though there was something in there he needed to tend to.

After Paul had left her wrist tape off, he left her unchained in the shed.

"You can go out if you want," he said to her, and smiled deceptively. She didn't trust his sudden change of mood. It was their third night in the forest, and Paul was essentially letting her go free. But she knew by now there was nowhere to run to, and so did he. The forest was even more dangerous at night, and she would never have found her way. Her feet were badly cut from when they'd arrived and walked in. She could hide, but she couldn't escape. "I'm using you as bait, you know," he informed her. "Sooner or later, your boyfriend is going to show up. He'll come looking for you, I can feel it, and when he finds you, I'll have him." His eyes looked mad as he said it.

"And then what?" she asked breathlessly.

"I'll kill him," Paul said with a wicked grin. "I

haven't decided yet what to do with you. I'm going to stay here, I'm never going back to prison."

"Maybe you can negotiate a reduced sentence." He looked intrigued by the suggestion for an instant. She was trying to distract him and seem sympathetic so he would trust her.

"I'd never thought about that. I could go back for a reduced sentence, but not for long. I won't go for another fourteen or fifteen years. I'd rather die here." He reminded her of when Charlie had debated about whether or not to go back to his real life. But Charlie had had greater incentive with two kids he wanted to see. Paul had none. He had no motivation whatsoever to become a model prisoner or get a better deal. He had no attachments at all that they could use as leverage. He had freedom here, like the birds in the nature preserve. This felt to him like his natural habitat, and he loved that there were no humans around. He didn't know how to handle them. When he was upset or angry or disappointed, or they interfered with him, he killed them.

Robert Bercy had confirmed to the police that they had seen Paul Pasquier at the Tronçais forest again, but that the chances of recapturing him were slim, given the difficulty accessing where he had located his camp. He had told them there was no sign of Aude. Charlie was discouraged that they hadn't

seen her, and afraid that he might already have disposed of her. Robert told him he doubted it. Paul
was too smart for that, and she could be a bargaining tool in case he needed one to escape, if they
found him.

"He's saving her to negotiate with. He knows he
might need her. He won't kill her yet. He's waiting
to see if he's safe here. And he's probably waiting
for you to show up," he said to Charlie. "He's more
likely to want to kill you than his ex-wife," Robert
said matter-of-factly. "The criminal mind is a won-
drous thing. It's all about who is the most useful to
them." What he said reminded Charlie of Isabelle,
in a more extreme version.

The police had assured Bercy that they had a
SWAT team ready to send in but wanted the opti-
mum time and conditions. They also wanted to
know if Aude was present, to warn their marksmen
if there was a hostage. Bercy watched closely but
didn't see her.

On the fourth day, the river was cold and the
weather was chilly, or Aude would have liked to go
swimming. She felt filthy, sleeping in the shed
every night, and being chained up for days. She'd
been wearing the same clothes since Pasquier kidnapped her. She suspected that the river was too
cold by now and the rapids too strong to risk it. She
might drown, which was appealing at times. Instead, she walked alongside the river, wondering
how long she would be there and if she'd survive.

The real world seemed more and more distant every day. This was her only reality now.

She was thinking about it, when Paul let her venture a little farther than usual on one of her riverbank walks. It was the only place where she didn't injure her bare feet on the sharp rocks and branches farther up near the cabin. She was lost in thought and desperate plans for escape, turning each one over in her mind, when she looked up and saw a man not far away in the forest. He was wearing forestry camouflage, like in the military, but she saw his face and he was looking straight at her. She didn't know whether to run toward him or away. He wasn't armed, and she knew now that Paul had an arsenal of rifles he'd concealed in his car. He'd brought several to his cabin. And if she ran to this man for help, and Paul killed him, he would chain her up forever. She didn't know if he was friend or foe, but either way, she doubted that he could help her. As he retreated slightly into the trees, he gave her a hand signal she didn't know, and put a finger to his lips for silence, which told her that he was there to help her and she was not to reveal his presence. She nodded and walked back toward the shed more swiftly than she'd come, so she didn't attract Paul's attention to the area where she had just been. Her heart nearly flew knowing that she wasn't alone in the forest. She didn't know if the man in camouflage had others with him, if he was from the police, the military, or some government agency, but he had seen her, and she had seen him, and she knew that his presence was a secret. It was the only shred of hope she'd had in four days.

Charlie had been standing just behind Bercy, but she hadn't seen him, and he had caught only a glimpse of her when she retreated. It was the information the police had been waiting for before they moved in on Pasquier with guns blazing. They didn't want to kill the hostage in the process. Now that they knew she was still alive they could plan accordingly. It was what they had needed to know. Bercy contacted them immediately.

"That was Aude." Charlie had whispered to Robert, so his voice didn't carry in the woods. Sometimes voices traveled a long way in nature. "That was her. She's alive!" He was shaking. It was the first evidence that Pasquier hadn't killed her, and what the police needed to know so they could rescue her.

"She is, and she saw me. The trick will be to get her out of here. This terrain is treacherous, and the forest is too dense to get any vehicles in. They'll have to send in a whole SWAT team to get her, and kill him. He won't come out of this alive," Robert predicted. The important thing was that she did. He knew the SWAT team would already be getting deployed as soon as they got the information that she was there. It had taken four days, which felt like a lifetime to Charlie.

He was elated to have gotten a glimpse of her, just as she was to have seen Robert, not even knowing who he was. But she could tell that he was on her side, and maybe part of a team searching for her. They had found her. Now all she had to do was reach them and get out safely, without Paul suspecting anything in the meantime.

Nothing happened that night. Bercy kept a close watch on Paul and saw him at the campfire. There was no sign of Aude again, and he guessed she might be in the shed.

The next day Paul told her he was out of food and had to go to the store. She'd been living on granola bars. He said he had none left, nor anything else for her, except water.

"How will we manage in winter?" she said innocently. "The snow must get deep here, and we have nowhere to store food. What if we get snowed in and can't get out?" It let him think that she was resigned to staying here with him, and believed she couldn't escape, so he relaxed and was less vigilant. He no longer taped her wrists or ankles, and hadn't chained her to the wall in the shed in several days. He thought he had her cowed by then, and too frightened to attempt an escape. She didn't know the reason, but he continued to treat her like a prisoner, not a sex slave, and she was grateful for that. He appeared to have no sexual interest in her at all. She was merely a hostage, and a potential bargaining tool if he needed one. His anger toward her seemed less acute. He got agitated when he spoke of their divorce, but if she didn't mention it now, he seemed calmer.

"We'll hunt what we eat in winter. I can snow-shoe out," he said practically. "You'll freeze to death if you try to escape then, so don't get any ideas. This is where you live now. It's the only home you have," he reminded her. She had seen him burn her house down, so she knew it was true. He was de-stroying her psychologically as well as physically, or wanted to. She nodded, seeming compliant. She was trying to convince him that she had accepted her situation and was no longer hoping to escape, as though this was a real life she could share with him. He appeared to be delusional about it. He ranted and raved at times, and hit her when he did.

He went to the store, and she remembered from the other times they'd been there that it was a long drive, and knew he'd be gone for an hour or even two. She noticed when he left that he forgot his phone on the table in the hut where he slept. He never let her enter. But he had left her free to walk around. All his rifles were lined up against one wall of his hut, near the window, fully loaded. She wouldn't dare to try to shoot him. She wouldn't know how. But after he left, she saw his phone on the table. She waited a few minutes to make sure he had left. She wasn't even sure if there was a signal, but she knew he went to his car daily to charge the phone, so she thought there must be, although she hadn't seen him use it. He had no one to call, and didn't want anyone to know where he was, or the police to trace him.

She walked quickly into the hut, grabbed the phone, and texted Charlie their location: "Near river, hut (him), shed (me), outhouse, just up from river. No shoes. I can't go far. Many rifles. Sometimes chained in shed. I love you." She sent it and erased the text message immediately, and prayed he wouldn't respond after Paul came back, if the text even got through. But the cell phone seemed to be working. She prayed that the signal would hold up. Charlie answered almost instantly. Bercy told him what to tell her. He had just heard from the police. They were coming in, but they needed time to devise a play.

"Run tonight toward where you saw us. As far as you can get. Police coming later. SWAT team to get you out. I love you. Be careful."

She texted back "You too," erased both messages, and replaced the phone in the exact position it had been in, and then ran back to her shed. It was chilly out, and she was cold with bare feet. The soles of her feet were a mess of infected cuts and lacerations now. She was thinking of Charlie's message. It was going around and around in her head. Run tonight . . . but to where? And how? And what if Paul chained her up again? She'd be trapped there in a blaze of gunfire in a showdown between Paul Pasquier and the police, and she knew Paul would fight to the death. He had nothing to lose. And she had Charlie to lose, which was everything to her. He was her world. And Pasquier her jailer. It seemed as though it would take a miracle to free her and for her and Charlie to both survive. Her heart was pounding furiously as she waited for Paul to come back from the store.

Chapter 13

Paul was gone for close to two hours. He came back from the grocery store with supplies, and she saw that he looked angry and was in a bad mood when he returned.

"I forgot my cell phone," he snarled at her, as if it was her fault.

"At the store?" she asked innocently. "Do you have to go back?"

"No, here," and then with no warning, he slapped her hard and she went reeling backwards and hit her head on the wall of the shed. He was enraged, mostly at himself for forgetting it, but he took it out on her. She touched her head and her fingers came away bloody. "You used it, didn't you, you bitch? Who did you call?" If she called the police, they'd have to go deeper into the forest, and he liked the camp where they were.

"Of course not. I didn't even know it was here," she said, looking offended.

"Did you call your boyfriend? Or the police?"

"No one, I swear. I don't go into your hut when you're not here. I didn't see it." He checked it thoroughly and found no suspicious messages, nothing he hadn't sent himself. He hadn't used it, so no one could track him. He wondered if she really had accepted her situation, and had given up all hope of escape. He could see the small patch of blood and hair matted at the back of her head. She had bruises all over from where he had struck her. He used her as a punching bag whenever he wanted, as a punishment, as a warning, for sins committed in the past, for divorcing him, for cheating on him, as he viewed it, for transgressions in the future that she hadn't even thought of. Her whole body, and face and arms and legs were black-and-blue.

"Well, don't ever touch it," he said again about his phone. He acted as if he was high on something and she wondered if he had bought drugs in town.

He shot a small bird that afternoon, and a rabbit, and cooked them himself after dark. As usual, he didn't offer her any, but he had bought her a ham sandwich at the grocery store, which was the biggest meal she'd had so far, but she couldn't eat that night, she was too nervous. She dropped it down one of the holes in the outhouse so he wouldn't notice, thanked him, and told him it was delicious. He didn't like wasting the food he hunted on her, and even less food that cost him money at the store. He'd been feeding her on snacks, sometimes a bag of pretzels or a bag of chips, which she made a meal of. All she wanted was to escape. She didn't care what she ate in the meantime.

He was quiet after he'd hit her that afternoon. He usually was after he lost his temper and slapped her around. She was never sure if it was exhaustion or remorse, probably most likely the former. He went into his hut that night as soon as he'd eaten. He had put his cell phone in his pocket, where it usually was. He seemed melancholy. She wondered if he was tired of the rustic discomforts of their life too. It was probably more comfortable living in prison than in the forest. And he would have to run for the rest of his life to stay out of prison. It seemed like a high price to pay for freedom. She had said as much to Charlie when he had been contemplating living the life of a dead man forever. But Paul had no home life to return to. All he had was prison, to atone for his crimes, or this, living like a caveman in the forest. In her opinion, there was no charm to it whatsoever, even for him, and in her case it included being chained up and beaten, if he felt like it.

He didn't bother to chain her that night, out of either negligence, laziness, or the belief that she couldn't escape. She had no idea what time it was. He had pawned her watch on the way, before they got to the forest, to buy food and sodas, which he

cooled in the river, with the milk he had bought.
She made a point of going into the shed and clos-
ing the door so he could hear it, waited a few minutes and then crept out. She stayed low, and tiptoed
across the cold earth, avoiding as many leaves and
broken branches as she could, to make no sound.
She headed straight into a thicket of bushes, and
past it, and ran as fast as she could on firm ground
and dirt and branches that cut her damaged feet.
She had no idea where she was going, but she tried
to run along the river, where she had seen the tall
man in camouflage. She hoped that he and his
team were somewhere around there, and that she
was running in the right direction. She stopped
several times, breathless, bent over to catch her
breath, and then dashed through the forest again,
hitting branches and trees and everything in her
path.

It felt like she'd been running for a long time
when she heard gunfire in the distance. She knew
it was Paul, and guessed that he had decided to
chain her up after all, and found her missing. She
could hear him in the distance, calling her name in
the forest. She couldn't outrun him, and he knew
the forest well. She was sure he would find her, and
instead of running, she hid in the thickest clump of
bushes she could find, curled up in a ball without
moving. The rifle fire came closer and then moved
farther away again. She didn't move. She just
stayed there and waited, and then she saw Paul's

car where he hid it and realized how far she'd gone. She had come a long way. She looked down and saw that the sleeve of her flannel shirt was torn and a piece of it was missing, caught on a bush some-where as she ran, and hoped that Paul didn't find it to lead him to her.

She knew she would hear gunfire again when the police came, maybe a lot of it. She decided not to move an inch until then. She didn't want to get lost, and didn't know her way in the forest, and didn't want to get caught in the crossfire or shot by mistake, or by Paul if he decided to kill her. She had no idea where the police were or when they were coming. All she'd had was Charlie's message to run. So she had, and now she was hiding.

The police had gathered at the outer edge of the forest. The police chief had come with the local sheriff, and a number of officers, and the SWAT team was waiting for orders from their captain. They were going in first with infrared masks, gog-gles, and equipment, so they could see any move-ment around them in the dark, nearby and at a distance. Robert Bercy introduced himself to the Chief of Police, and confirmed that they had seen Aude walking along the river yesterday, and had signaled to her. And they had exchanged a brief text message with her that day and told her that help was on the way and to run that night, if she could.

"I didn't know she had a cell phone with her," the police chief said.

"She doesn't," Charlie informed him. "She used Pasquier's, and hopefully erased everything before he came back. I think he was out and must have left his phone."

"Signals are erratic here. You're lucky you got through. There's a signal tower just beyond the forest, but if they were any further in, they couldn't access the signal."

They had all heard the gunshots earlier, and weren't sure what it indicated, but the SWAT team's instructions were clear. Free the hostage and shoot to kill the hostage taker if necessary. It was Aude they were trying to save, not Paul Pasquier. She'd been gone for five days, which had seemed like an eternity to Charlie, and she wasn't out yet.

Shortly after eleven P.M., the SWAT team got their orders. After waiting for a signal from the head of the SWAT team once they were in, the police were authorized to come in behind them with guns blazing. They wanted it to be fast and effective.

"You may come across the hostage on your way in," Bercy told them. "We advised her to run tonight, if she could. We don't know if he has her tied up or in chains or what. She texted us that he's in the hut, she's in the shed, and there's an outhouse.

So they need to watch out for the shed." It was all helpful information. The Chief of Police ordered Robert and Charlie to hang back, and they did as they were told. The police didn't want civilians underfoot or getting hurt, even experienced ones like Bercy, whose gun was visible at his side. It was a meticulously orchestrated operation. And it nearly killed Charlie to be forced to wait on the perimeter for news, but Robert told him it was essential. They might inadvertently get in the way, interfere, and foil the attempt to save her, which was the last thing they wanted. They had found her, which was a miracle in itself, and now trained expert teams were going to free her from her insane ex-husband, and take him back to prison, if he lived, or kill him to save her.

The SWAT team left, crouching and making their way silently deeper into the forest. They went past where Aude was hiding without being aware of her presence, or she of theirs, they were so silent. They reached the little cluster of small buildings ten minutes later. The hut was surrounded, two of the SWAT team broke down the door, and were instantly face-to-face with Pasquier, who greeted them with a blaze from his automatic rifle. He missed them, and they shot him in the leg, and crushed him to the floor while the rest of the team stormed the buildings, looking for Aude. Paul Pasquier was writhing in pain and cursing them, with his rifle clutched next to him until they grabbed it seconds later. The other members of the team came back to report that the shed was unoccupied and there was no one in the outhouse either. They searched and didn't find her anywhere in the clearing or the area.

"She ran away tonight. She's out there somewhere," Pasquier said. He wanted them to find her so he could kill her, and hoped he still would. She deserved it.

The leader of the SWAT team was holding Pasquier to the floor with his full weight. He hated men like him who preyed on the weak and innocent, and terrorized them, and made hostages of people, risking their lives and too often killing them. And the police still didn't know Aude's whereabouts, what Pasquier had done to her, and what condition she was in. She was cowering in the bushes, shaking, as the police ran past her with floodlights and spotlights. Everyone in the second wave was aware via radio that the brief gunfire had stopped and the hostage taker had been subdued. What remained to happen was to find Aude. She left her hiding place in the shrubbery and walked back to the small compound. With the police spotlights focused on the hut and the shed, she could see what was happening. The police and the SWAT team were swarming over the area, looking for her.

Aude headed back toward the shed then, as fast as she could in bare feet over the rough terrain. She stumbled once and caught herself, and a moment later she was in their midst, waving, and they recognized her immediately. Charlie and Robert Bercy had just joined the fray and brought up the rear. They weren't an interference risk now. The action was over, except for locating her.

Aude got there in time to see two members of the SWAT team drag Paul out of the hut. He saw her at the same time and screamed at her from the distance.

"You bitch! You're a whore!" And before anyone could stop him, Pasquier had slipped a hand into a hidden pocket of his army surplus pants, pulled out a small handgun they hadn't found, and aimed it straight at Aude. Charlie let out a shout and ran toward her to protect her, but one of the marksmen shot Paul Pasquier before he could pull the trigger. He was dead before he hit the ground, and all hell broke loose as Charlie ran toward Aude and held her in his arms. Paul had almost killed her after all. If Paul hadn't shouted and the police hadn't acted as fast as they did, she would have been dead at that moment. Charlie was crying as he held her, and she clung to him. It had been the longest five days of their lives. But it was over. She had lost her home and everything in it, but not her life.

When he pulled away from her, in the bright police lights flooding the area, Charlie was shocked at the condition of her face. She had been badly battered, and her face was nothing compared to her body, which he hadn't seen yet.

"Oh my God, Aude . . ." He gently touched the cuts and bruises on her face. Pasquier had hit her hard "to teach her a lesson." She had marks on her arms from the chains, and the soles of her feet had deep cuts.

Pasquier's body was removed quickly. The police asked her if she had any belongings she wanted to take with her, and she said she had none. She was just grateful to get out alive. There were at least thirty people clustered around the small buildings she'd been imprisoned in. Crowded into the clearing, they took photos of the area, radioed to their base that the hostage was safe, and then made their way slowly back the way they came. Once they got as far as the road that led to the forest, they brought an ambulance for Aude. She said she didn't need it, but they wanted her to use it to go to the hospital. Charlie climbed in with her, and Bercy followed behind in his SUV.

Aude was still in a daze from everything that had happened, and she and Charlie talked softly on the way. She was so grateful to see him, to be free and to be alive, and he just wanted to hold her and feel her near him after five days of terror that Paul would kill her or that Charlie would never see her again. Paul had almost gotten her in the end. And now he was dead.

"He wasn't like that when I met him, until later," she explained to Charlie. "He was even worse now. He was completely crazy. The only reason he didn't kill me was that he was saving me as bait for you. He wanted to kill you too," she said. She was shaking in his arms, and he was shocked at how she looked, filthy and beaten.

Charlie was with her when the nurses helped her undress at the hospital. They cut away her clothes. The bruising was horrific, on her cheeks, her face, her back, her arms, her legs, her breasts, and on her stomach, where he had kicked her, they could see the outline of the sole of his boot. Her entire body had been battered, and her mind. She had never lived through as much trauma and terror, convinced that he was going to kill her, completely at his mercy, and unable to stop him. She had been alone in the forest with him and would have been totally helpless if he had made up his mind to kill her, shoot her, beat her to death. There was a psychiatrist waiting to talk to her at the hospital, who found her in better shape than he expected. He normally treated victims who were held prisoner for months or even years. She had held up remarkably well for five nightmarish days.

Charlie thought it was much worse than what he'd gone through, going over the cliff. That had been truly an accident, terrifying in its own way, but not the same as someone intentionally hurting Aude and wanting to kill her, for many days. He wondered how she would ever feel safe at home again, although he fully intended to see to it that she would, wherever she lived with him. And he hoped that in time, the terrifying memories would fade.

Robert Bercy left them at the hospital, and Charlie thanked him profusely for his expertise, his kindness, his devotion to the job. Charlie and Aude had been in the hands of experts with Robert and the SWAT team that had subdued and ultimately killed Paul, and saved her in the end from Paul's last crazed attempt to kill her. Paul didn't want her to survive, he wanted only to punish her. It was hard to believe she'd ever known him and been married to him. It was an experience Charlie and Aude knew they'd never forget.

The doctor at the hospital wanted Aude to spend the night, but Aude wanted to leave and staying wouldn't make a difference to her bruises, which would take time to heal. The nurses and doctor had bandaged her lacerated and infected feet, and were sending her home in hospital pajamas and paper slippers. They had thrown her clothes away. Charlie was wearing camouflage gear Bercy had given him. She said she wanted to go home, and then she looked at Charlie sadly.

"I don't have a home anymore, do I?"

He shook his head. He had seen the cabin after the fire, and she'd only seen it when Paul started it. It was bad enough then. "There's nothing left," he said gently. "You can pick through the ashes, and maybe there's something you want and can salvage." But he had seen himself how little was left.

"My paintings must be gone, even the portrait of you," she said. She had loved it.

"You can paint another one. There's only one you, and you survived. That's all I care about." He couldn't keep his hands off her. He just wanted to hold her and protect her.

"So where shall we stay?" she asked Charlie, as they left the hospital nearest the forest, where she'd been taken. It was two-thirty in the morning, and Charlie had just arranged for a car and driver to take them to their rented beach cottage, which they had taken as refuge from Paul Pasquier when he first escaped. They would be safe everywhere now. But neither of them had a fixed home. He had been hotel-hopping in Paris, since Isabelle was living in the apartment he wanted back, and Aude's old cabin had been burned to the ground. So all they had was the rented cottage in Équemauville for the time being, and it was cozy and nice, even if it wasn't home.

They got to the beach cottage at eight in the morning, and Aude could barely make it up the front steps. Charlie carried her the rest of the way. She had a terrible déjà vu when she saw the kitchen, of when she had turned and seen Paul standing there, of when the nightmare began after he let himself into the cottage and found her alone. She knew it was going to take her a long time to forget that image. It was when he had chloroformed her, tied her up with duct tape, and put her in the trunk of his car. She was shaking when they walked in, and Charlie gently put her to bed, and lay with her, holding her gently until she fell asleep. He kept telling her that she was safe now, but she knew it would be a long time before she felt safe again.

Later that morning, Charlie called Armand to tell him that Aude was home and safe, and he called Philippe Delacroix, his attorney, to tell him the same, and thank him for the referral to Robert Bercy, who had been extraordinary.

"He's amazing, isn't he?" Philippe said. "And I'm glad your friend is all right."

"He was fantastic. I want to have lunch with him sometime. How are the Spousal Wars going, by the way?" He hadn't talked to Philippe in a week while they searched for Aude, after the depositions. It was hard to believe it had only been a week, the longest of his life.

"Isabelle's a stubborn woman. You had guts marrying her. I think we're getting close to a settlement number, but we're not done yet. The minute we get her to lower one number, she raises another. The concept of compromise and trade-off is not familiar to her," Philippe said, and Charlie laughed ruefully.

"That sounds like her," Charlie said. "She's a master negotiator, she learned it from her father. He's a killer in business." It was what she had wanted him to be, and he never was.

"Maybe another week or two," Philippe said optimistically, "and then we'll be done."

Charlie and Aude talked about her five days in the forest, and then she needed to talk about something else less traumatic. "What are you and Isabelle actually fighting about?" Aude asked him. She was exhausted and resting in bed, and he brought her meals. She had never wanted to be intrusive and ask him details about the divorce. She knew it had something to do with real estate and investments, but she didn't know more than that, didn't think it was her place and didn't want to pry. Charlie had been discreet about it.

"It's long and complicated and fairly absurd. I gave her a château, and I'm more than happy to make that official. She can have the château. It was in my will, so for now she owns it. She loves it. And I want our Paris apartment, which has a gorgeous view, lots of space, the Eiffel Tower right in the backyard, and enough bedrooms for everyone. And that's just the beginning. I bought all the real estate in the first place. Then she needs to return the pension that my job paid her. She's not entitled to it, since I'm not dead. And the remaining part of the drama is that she inherited twenty-five percent of my investments and assets, and I want to split it in half with her, so we have money to live on. She wants the château, the apartment, most of my assets, and to keep the pension of a man who is not dead. In other words, she wants everything, even though I'm still alive now." He could see a look of panic on Aude's face as he said it. He had never been as detailed with her before.

"Wait a minute. You have a château, and an apartment in Paris, which I now assume isn't small, and investments, and you lived in a rented cabin with me for almost five months? Charlie, I'm a poor artist, and I don't even have the cabin now. I have nothing. I don't even have underwear or shoes, they all burned up. What are you doing with me, and how are you going to be happy with a woman who has nothing?"

"Right now, Isabelle doesn't have much either, which is why she wants everything that's mine, and why I'm giving her the château." He said it as though he had said, "I'm giving her the toaster," or the kitchen table. "She's going to inherit from her father one day too. So she'll be fine." He wasn't worried about Isabelle.

"Charlie, I've never even been in a château, let alone owned one or lived in one. How are you going to be happy with me?" She looked devastated. She had nothing to give him except herself, which was all he wanted. He wanted nothing from her except her love.

"That's one of the many things I love about you," he said softly. "You don't give a damn about any of that. Isabelle would rather have me dead and own it all. And she'd much rather have the château than our marriage. She loved what I gave her, what I could buy her. I don't think she ever even knew who I was, or cared. Besides, I'm going to be much poorer now when she's through with me. She's doing a very good job of that. I love you, in a cabin, in a château, in a cottage at the beach, in a tent. And I want you to come and live with me in the apartment when I get it back, and I will get it back. It's only fair since she'll have the château."

"Are you sure?" She looked worried. "I'm not too plain for you?"

"Don't forget, I wanted to stay and never go back to that life, and I wanted to let them think I was dead. None of that is important to me. *You* are."

"I'll embarrass you. Your friends will think I'm some peasant out of nowhere."

"You're not a peasant, you're a very talented artist. And I have no idea what I am now. I'm unemployed. Maybe I'll go back and work for Armand, and you can be married to a mechanic. How does that sound? Is that plain enough for you?" She was smiling at him. He made it all sound easy, and as though owning a château was normal and the transition would be a breeze.

"You're crazy. If you had told me you owned a château, I would never have let you into my house the night you went off the cliff."

"Don't be such a snob," he teased her.

"I want to see the apartment. Maybe it's too fancy for me." She suspected it would be.

"Then you'll have to get used to it. And I want to build you a studio to paint in, in the apartment."

"Don't you want someone fancier, from your own world?" She was serious and he shook his head.

"That's what I wanted to run away from. I'm in love with you, not your job, or your house, or where you come from, or what you do. And I hope you can say the same about me, that you can love me even if I have a big apartment. And what do you have against big apartments?"

"They're not cozy."

"Ours will be because we'll be in it." She liked the way he said it, and he kissed her. It was such a relief to be home with him. It felt like a miracle to both of them. "Now shut up and enjoy it," he said, and she laughed, but hearing about the château had been a shock. She was glad he was giving it to his ex-wife. Aude didn't want one. "We'll have to live at the beach cottage for a while, by the way, because Isabelle has a month to move out of the apartment. Or we can stay at a hotel."

"The Ritz, I assume," she teased him, and he nodded.

"If you want, although that's a little fancy for me."

"I was just kidding!" she said, looking worried again. They were wonderful problems to have after what she'd been through. It pained him to see the bruises on her face. And it was a relief to her to talk about normal life and their future, and even his divorce, after fearing for her life for five days. She needed the distraction.

"We'll have to give you lessons in how to enjoy being spoiled by a man who loves you," Charlie said to her, and cradled her in his arms. Aude had been in no way prepared for who Charlie had turned out to be after he walked into her cottage the night he fell off a cliff and nearly drowned. It had felt like their destiny that night, and despite the trappings that unnerved her, she still believed it was. And now destiny had saved her. They had both survived.

She sank into the pillows and slept for the rest of the day, while Charlie watched her, more grateful than he had ever been in his life. He knew that it would take Aude time to heal after the ordeal she'd been through, and she had agreed to see a therapist, which seemed smart to both of them. But the important thing was that she had survived. Paul hadn't killed her. She was alive and so was Charlie after the accident in June. And they had both been reminded of what mattered in life, not châteaux or big jobs, or even the cabin she loved. They had each other, and that was enough.

Chapter 14

It took another three weeks to get Isabelle to sign the divorce settlement on the terms Charlie wanted, which everyone, even her lawyer, agreed were reasonable and fair. Isabelle was the only one who thought she should have both the château *and* the apartment.

"You can buy an apartment you want, for heaven's sake," Charlie told her in exasperation. "I'm giving you enough money to buy a great apartment in any neighborhood in Paris!" She acknowledged that it was true, she just felt that Charlie "owed" it to her to give her what she wanted, which was exactly what he had run away from. She felt entitled to everything and she had to give nothing back in return. It was a perfect arrangement for her, and never had been for him.

He was happy with Aude now, and the two

women couldn't have been more different. As soon as Isabelle moved out of the apartment, taking most of the art and all of the furniture with her, which he didn't argue about, in order to keep the peace, he took Aude to see it.

She was shocked at how big it was. It was five thousand square feet of elegance with a spectacular terrace, a lovely garden, and the Eiffel Tower practically in their backyard. Charlie loved it, and Aude promised to try to adjust to it. She said she'd get a map so she could find her way around, and a compass. She was the opposite of Isabelle in every way, which he loved about her. He loved everything about her, and he couldn't wait to move in with her. He told her to decorate however she wanted. There were several little-known artists she loved, and she introduced him to their work. She didn't want anything to impress people with. She wanted things because they loved them. And the studio he wanted to build for her was going to be gorgeous, with a view of the garden and the Eiffel Tower.

Isabelle was busy looking at apartments in the best neighborhoods in Paris. She and Stephanie were having a ball doing it. Isabelle was spending a lot of time on her new beau's boat, and discovering the world of yachting, which she thoroughly enjoyed.

For the moment, Aude and Charlie were commuting between their rented beach cottage and various hotels when they came to the city. It was going to take three months to have his apartment painted and to buy new furniture they were picking out together, so it looked as cozy as Aude wanted. They were educating each other in new ways. The apartment would be completely different with her in it. And she was recovering well from the ordeal with Paul, with the help of a therapist.

At the same time, Charlie was talking to people he knew about a job. He wanted to go back to publishing, but not at the level he'd been at before. He didn't want all the headaches that went with being a CEO, he wanted to be a senior editor. He had been reading voraciously to become familiar with new authors and current books. He'd gotten lazy about keeping up.

During the thirteen years since he walked out as CEO, he had matured, and past sins had been forgiven. He got an offer from a publishing house he loved. It represented authors he respected, and they would never open a hard or soft porn division. He accepted the job, they were thrilled to have him, and he couldn't wait to start after the New Year. The apartment wouldn't be finished yet, and he and Aude would be camping out in it for a while until all the changes were complete.

The salary he was going to make as a senior editor was more modest than as CEO, and a fraction of what Jerome Jansen had paid him in the plastics industry. But he no longer had a father-in-law he had to impress, or a wife who had a voracious appetite for anything expensive so she could impress her friends. And as senior editor, he could work at home as much of the time as he wanted, which appealed to him too. He could edit manuscripts while Aude painted, and they would be there together. They were inseparable now, while Aude recovered.

They were enjoying the beach cottage while they still had it, and were thinking about renting a different one in the summer, something his kids might enjoy. They had discussed it and Olivier and Judith liked the idea. And in the meantime, Charlie and Aude were walking on the beach in winter and loving being together. Their time together was part of the healing process for Aude.

Once Charlie had his publishing job squared away, he went up to see Armand at the garage and make him a proposition he was excited about. He hoped Armand would be too. He wanted to invest in the garage, and help Armand modernize his business practices, as long as he would let Charlie work there occasionally. He told Armand it was the best job he'd ever had, the most fun, and even his new job in publishing wouldn't come close to it. Armand was bowled over by the offer, and happy with the influx of money. He had loved working with Charlie too. They shook hands on the deal for an amount that was modest for Charlie, and he told Aude about it that night.

"I made a great deal today," he told her over dinner in one of his favorite bistros. He hated fancy restaurants. Isabelle had always insisted on them, the fancier the better. Alain Ducasse, La Tour d'Argent, Lasserre, Taillevent. Charlie was always more at ease in the old Parisian bistros, where they served real French bistro food and all his favorite recipes. Aude liked them better too.

"So what was the deal?" she asked him. "Please tell me you didn't buy a château." She looked genuinely worried.

"I know it will make you very happy when I tell you I can no longer afford one." She looked relieved. "Neither can my ex-wife, in the style in which she's been entertaining, but she hasn't figured that out yet, and it's no longer my problem. I invested in Armand's garage today. He needs help, and we are now partners, and he's going to let me work there on weekends, whenever I want to." She laughed and he was beaming. The two men had become good friends, and Charlie still loved working on cars and was good at it.

"Congratulations," she said, and they toasted his new partnership with a bottle of good wine.

They had another big event coming up. Charlie had returned from the dead six weeks before, and both of his children had been too busy in their jobs to come home at first. And Charlie had been away while Aude was taken hostage. He had long talks with Judith and Olivier on the phone, but he hadn't seen them yet. They were both coming to Paris now to celebrate their father being back. He wanted Aude to meet them, and they were curious about her. They had met their mother's new boyfriend, Yves Napier, and weren't sure about him, but liked his boat. He seemed very old to them.

They had agreed that their father would have dinner with them, and Aude would join them for dessert. He wanted time alone with them to discuss the divorce, and explain why he had disappeared after the accident, and had taken so long to come back, and had even considered not coming back at all, which would have been a big mistake. Aude was right.

He wanted to have time with them to answer their questions and speak freely without a stranger present, which Aude was to them. She understood and was nervous about meeting them, and he hoped that they would understand why he loved her. He had been very gracious about their mother and hadn't said anything critical about her. She hadn't been as gracious about him, but that was up to her. He couldn't lead life to please her anymore. It had almost destroyed him. His children didn't need to know that, but he did. He was fully aware now of all the things that had gone wrong in their marriage, and hoped not to make the same mistakes with Aude, whether married or not. They hadn't figured out their plans yet, and the divorce wouldn't be final for a year, which gave them time.

It would be hard to repeat the same errors with
Aude. The two women were so different, and he
was different now too. He'd been honest with himself and both women about where he'd gone wrong.
Isabelle was only too happy to assign all the blame
to him.

She was talking about getting married again as
soon as she could to Yves, and talked incessantly
about his boat and his plane. She wanted to marry
him for all the wrong reasons, in Charlie's opinion.
All the material trappings were of great importance
to her, more than the person, and Stephanie agreed
with her. She thought Isabelle's new man was fabulous because he had a great deal of money. Charlie
wanted more out of life than that, and now he had
it with Aude.

The dinner with his children went even better than
he'd hoped. Olivier asked more questions about the
divorce than his sister, because she was younger
and assumed that her father was right in all things.
Olivier, at twenty-nine, was trying to figure out
who he was and who he wanted to become. "It
doesn't bother you, Dad, that you'll have a less important job now than you did before, and you won't
be a CEO?" Olivier wanted to climb the ladder to
success, and it confused him that his father was
heading down, and was happy about it.

"Not at all. I did that, twice. I was the CEO of

two companies. I loved one job and hated the other. I blew the first one and escaped the second. At this point I don't want the pressure and all the responsibility on my shoulders. It comes at a high price. If I were younger, I'd probably do it again. If I were your age, I'm sure I would. But right now, I want to breathe. I want to do work I love and I'm proud of and that is meaningful to me. I want to feel good about myself and my life when I go to bed at night. I don't need to impress anybody. I'm doing it for me. I'm lucky because I'm with a woman now who doesn't care so much about those things." Isabelle had been all about appearances, which he didn't say to them. Aude was a woman of substance, with solid values she and Charlie shared.

"Do you miss Mom?" Judith asked him cautiously.

"Sometimes. We had a really good time together for a long time, when we were both young. And then we both got different. Too different, and it didn't work anymore. We just couldn't be married anymore. Sometimes people change. We both did."

It took Olivier a long time to ask the question, but it was an important one they needed the answer to. "Why did you take so long to come back after the accident, and let us think you were dead? Judith and I were heartbroken, and I think Mom was too, although she's too proud to show it." Charlie didn't entirely agree with Olivier's analysis of his mother, but that wasn't the point.

"I was so unhappy with what I'd done with my life, my job, my career, my relationship with your mom. I didn't know how to do it differently or how to stop it. And suddenly I had a chance to start over, to be someone else, to be myself and lead a different life, have a new identity. I thought that was the way to do it, but it wasn't. I wanted to become someone else, to disappear without a trace. Maybe we all feel that at some point in our lives when things go wrong and we want to run away. That was how I felt that night when I almost drowned.

"But what I needed to do was still be me, and do things differently. I needed to be honest with myself and everyone else. I had to figure out how to be me, the way I wanted to be, not be what everyone else wanted me to be. It took me a while to figure that out. I shouldn't have tried to run away and stayed away for so long, and I apologize to you both for it. I always knew I'd come back to you. I wasn't going to abandon you. But I had to figure out who I was before I came home, or the rest of my life would be worthless." Olivier nodded. It made more sense to him now, and to Judith too. They had never realized how unhappy he'd been. "I'm happy to be home now, and pretending to be dead was a stupid thing to do. I'm really sorry for the pain I caused you, and your mom," he said. "I want to be part of your lives, spend time with you when you want to, work at a job I love, enjoy my life, and be with a woman who has the same ideals and goals and principles I do. If you don't have that, marriage can be very hard. Your mom and I weren't that different when we got married, but we are now.

"It's what Judith said to me a long time ago. I like being plain and your mom likes being fancy." All three of them laughed at that and how true it was.

"She's getting very fancy now," Judith commented. "Her new boyfriend has a big boat he keeps in Monaco, and a plane that seats ten people."

"Maybe he'll buy her an airline," Charlie said, and they all laughed. "Or a cruise ship."

"Stephanie says Mom should marry him," Judith volunteered, "because he has so much money. She says that it doesn't matter that he's really old. He might die and leave her all his money since he has no children."

"That's who I didn't want to be when I grow up," Charlie said pensively.

"It might be nice for Mom though. She can buy anything she wants," Judith said. She and Olivier had to figure out their own values in time. Charlie knew that all he could do was share his with them, and ultimately they would pick and choose what they wanted, and become their own people, with their own goals for their lives. He hoped they'd be wiser than he had been.

*   *   *

They went to meet Aude at the Bar Vendôme at the Hôtel Ritz after dinner. It was very chic. The décor was very old-school and traditional, and very luxurious and beautiful. The Ritz was very grand. There was a pianist playing soft music. Aude looked slightly intimidated when she met them, more because of the opulent surroundings than the children. Judith was warm and friendly right from the beginning, and Olivier was more reserved and needed time to get to know her, but warmed up as the evening wore on and they talked. She was a genuinely nice person and it showed.

Inevitably, they talked about the accident, since it was how she and Charlie had met. She said that their dad looked like the Loch Ness Monster when he arrived on her doorstep that night and was very badly banged up. It had been a big accident, and a miracle that he had survived. A miracle and a blessing, and she said she was very grateful that he did survive it, and they were together now. Charlie didn't want them thinking that she had broken up his marriage, which really wasn't the case. He and Isabelle had done that themselves, and he admitted it to his children.

Aude talked to them about being an artist, which she really loved doing, and going to the Beaux-Arts when she was younger. They talked about art and work, and accidents and people, and their jobs in London and New York. The rest of the evening went by quickly, and they laughed a lot, and were comfortable together when they left the Ritz. Aude said that she hoped that they would like what she and their dad were doing to the apartment. They were putting in a home cinema, which the children liked a lot, and a gym, and a sauna because Charlie wanted one. Aude wanted the house to be friendly and fun for all of them. Judith and Olivier liked what they heard and could hardly wait to see the apartment. They were staying with their mother, in a temporary apartment she had rented, while they were in Paris. Isabelle was looking for a new one to buy with Yves. But as soon as their old apartment was ready, the children wanted to stay with their dad and Aude too. She told them that they would both have their old rooms, with all their things in them. When she and Charlie dropped them off at their mother's they all hugged and kissed.

"Thanks for all the explanations, Dad," Olivier said. "Now I think I get it. It must have been hard to come back to a lot of things you weren't happy about, your job, and all the rest of it, that you didn't know how to change." They were being very generous with him.

"Sometimes you just have to be brave and face up to things. And sometimes it's damn hard to do. I should have done it sooner. The more you deal with, and the more honest you are with yourself and the people in your life, the less mess you make. I made a big mess with that accident, and not coming home right away, but I was lucky. Good things came of it and it all worked out." He wasn't afraid to admit it now, and Aude could see that his son and daughter respected him for his honesty. She admired Charlie for how he had handled it with them, and she had enjoyed meeting them. They were both so young, and had a long way to go. She didn't envy them the messes and mistakes that they would make. She had made some very big ones herself, like Paul Pasquier. But Judith and Olivier were lucky to have Charlie. He was an honest man, and a good father. It gave them a great head start in life, which she hadn't had, losing her parents so young. And Charlie wasn't afraid to admit his mistakes and his frailties to his children, to her, or himself.

As they drove back to the hotel where they were staying she leaned over and kissed him.

"Your kids are great. I told you that you'd come back to them in the end, because you're an honest man and a brave one. It would have been cowardly if you'd just disappeared without a trace, and you're not a coward." She said it with conviction. She was proud of him.

"It was so tempting, but in the end, I just couldn't do it. You were right. I'd miss them too much anyway. Thank you for meeting them tonight." He glanced at her warmly. He was proud of her too.

"I enjoyed it," she said, smiling at him. "I liked the Ritz too." She laughed guiltily as she admitted it.

"Watch out . . . that's pretty fancy . . ." She gave him a shove and they laughed, going into their hotel. The best part of the accident was the time they had spent getting to know each other when he stayed with her, and now he was with a woman he admired and respected and loved being with. And she felt the same way about him. They had been through the fires of hell and come out stronger and more in love than ever. He couldn't think of anything better.

Chapter 15

Charlie drove to Normandy to see his new business partner the next day. Armand was having his morning coffee at the garage when Charlie got there. They talked about the state of the world, the current government, an upcoming election, business at the garage, and their respective kids. Two of Armand's daughters were making life choices that worried him, but the other two were doing well, which was about par for most people's kids, Charlie's too, although for the moment he was happy and proud of both of them. They were doing well at their jobs and liked the cities they lived in. He told Armand that their introduction to Aude the night before had gone smoothly.

"She's a good woman," Armand confirmed. "Has she gotten over the trauma of that nightmare with her ex-husband?"

"I think so. She doesn't like to talk about it. I can't blame her. At least it's over and she's safe now." In fact, she was recovering surprisingly well.

When they finished their coffee, Charlie grabbed his overalls from a hook on the wall and put them on over his jeans and sweatshirt as Armand smiled at him.

"I like having a partner. I never thought we'd be in business together when I gave you a job after the accident. I thought you were running from the law or something."

"I was just running from myself." Armand nodded and they both got to work. Charlie left the garage at six o'clock to meet Aude at the beach cottage for dinner. He promised to come back the following weekend, and Armand waved when he left. It had been a good day. Charlie had done three sets of brakes.

As he drove the familiar road, past the place where he'd gone off the cliff to his near death below, Charlie glanced at the drop and wondered, as he always did now, how he had survived it, and how he'd thought he could walk out of his life and never go back, and just disappear without a trace. It had been so tempting at times, just to run away. He was glad now he hadn't, that he had Aude in his life to love, and Armand as a friend, a new job as an editor, and, when he wanted it, as a car mechanic.

It had all worked out perfectly, the way it was

meant to. He would have missed all of it, or the best parts, if he had disappeared forever. He was happy he hadn't, as he drove through Normandy to the woman who had bandaged his wounds that night and had turned out to be the love of his life. You just never knew how things would work out, and what might happen. Charlie was living proof of that. Six months later, he had never felt more alive. Everything in his life had changed in ways he couldn't even have imagined. He was happy and so was Aude, and despite the traumas they had gone through, there was so much to be grateful for. Courage was always the right answer. And love, the reward.

About the Author

DANIELLE STEEL has been hailed as one of the world's bestselling authors, with a billion copies of her novels sold. Her many international bestsellers include *Second Act, Happiness, Palazzo, The Wedding Planner, Worthy Opponents, Without a Trace, The Whittiers, The High Notes,* and other highly acclaimed novels. She is also the author of *His Bright Light,* the story of her son Nick Traina's life and death; *A Gift of Hope,* a memoir of her work with the homeless; *Expect a Miracle,* a book of her favorite quotations for inspiration and comfort; *Pure Joy,* about the dogs she and her family have loved; and the children's books *Pretty Minnie in Paris* and *Pretty Minnie in Hollywood.*

daniellesteel.com
Facebook.com/DanielleSteelOfficial
Twitter: @daniellesteel
Instagram: @officialdaniellesteel

Look for The Ball at Versailles,
coming soon in hardcover

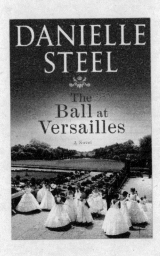

Four American debutantes attend a renowned
Paris cotillion in #1 *New York Times* bestselling
author Danielle Steel's captivating new novel.

Chapter 1

Jane Fairbanks Alexander saw the creamy white envelope sitting on the silver tray on the table in the entrance hall, where the part-time housekeeper who came three times a week had put it. Gloria was Irish and had worked for them daily when Jane's daughter Amelia was still in school, but now that she was in college, Jane didn't need Gloria as often and she had another part-time job the other two days of the week. She bought the groceries she knew Jane liked, did the laundry, and cleaned the apartment. Amelia only came home now for the occasional weekend. It was her freshman year at Barnard. The apartment seemed strangely quiet without her. It was small, neat, and elegant, and had two bedrooms, in a prewar building in Manhattan on Fifth Avenue and Seventy-sixth Street, with a doorman, which made Jane feel safe. On the days that Gloria was there, it was nice for Jane to come home to a clean, tidy apartment, with her laundry neatly folded on her bed. Having an orderly home was some slight compensation for the fact that Amelia wasn't there anymore. She was uptown in the dorm. Barnard was the female sister school of Columbia University.

Amelia was loving her freshman year. She was an English literature major, which made sense since Jane was the second-in-command of a venerable publishing house in the city. Amelia's father had been in publishing too, and Amelia had clear goals. She wanted to go to law school when she graduated from Barnard, and hoped to get into Columbia, which had been one of the first law schools to accept women. For the past nine years, Jane had brought Amelia up on her own. She had been nine years old when her father, Alfred, died. She had never known him as her mother had. Jane had warm memories of him before the war, when he was still a whole person, before he had gone to war and everything had changed.

Jane had met him when she was a junior at Vassar. He had been getting a masters in English at Yale. Once they met at a deb ball in New York, he had courted her for a year and a half and traveled from New Haven to visit her in Poughkeepsie as often as he was able. They got engaged during her senior year, and married as soon as she graduated, in 1939. Alfred was twenty-four then, and Jane was twenty-two. He had an entry-level job in publishing at G. P. Putnam's, and he had a bright future ahead of him. He had started as an editorial assistant and was rapidly promoted to junior editor. He loved his job and looked forward to being a senior editor or even editor in chief one day.

Jane got a job fresh out of college, working at *Life* magazine as an assistant copy editor. Their interests had always been very similar and they both loved their jobs in publishing. Alfred was assigned to the more literary books, and the manuscripts he worked on were loftier than the work Jane did at *Life*. But her work was lively, fun, and she found it exciting. She got pregnant three months after they married and had an easy pregnancy. She was at the magazine for a year, until she gave birth to Amelia in the summer of 1940, and never went back to work after that. She was happy staying home with their baby daughter and caring for her herself, and Alfred's job, along with the money he had inherited, provided them with a very pleasant life. He didn't expect her to go back to work.

Alfred didn't have a great deal of money, but his grandparents had left him a handsome bequest that provided some luxuries as well as necessities. And later, after his parents died, one of cancer and the other of a stroke, they had left him some more money too. He still had to work, but he and Jane weren't dependent on his job, and it was comforting to know that they had a tiny amount of savings in the bank, invested safely and conservatively. Their backgrounds were very similar. Jane's father was the president of a bank in New York, and her mother was from a distinguished family in Boston. She came from "old money" too. Jane's parents were from families that had once been more comfortable than they were now. They had lost most of their fortune in the Crash of '29, but there was still enough left to provide their heirs with a comfortable, secure life. Alfred's family were part of the Old Guard of New York. He had several cousins who had more money than he did, but his was among the best-known names of New York Society. He was by no means the richest among them, but he had enough to support his wife and daughter and there was no need for Jane to work. Alfred's father was an investment banker on Wall Street, and like Jane's mother, Alfred's mother had never worked.

The two sets of parents knew each other. Alfred's and Jane's fathers belonged to the same club, where they often met after work, and both their mothers volunteered once a week together as Gray Ladies for the Red Cross. It was work they enjoyed. They liked sharing a granddaughter once Amelia was born and took her to the park together sometimes to see the animals at the zoo or ride on the carousel. Jane and Alfred were only children, so Amelia's arrival was met with wonder and delight by both sets of grandparents.

Jane and Alfred's lives rolled along smoothly from the moment they married for two and a half years, until Amelia was eighteen months old. At night they talked about Alfred's job, his progress and latest promotions, and the manuscripts he was assigned to work on. But when Pearl Harbor was hit, Alfred enlisted within days afterwards. It was a few months before he shipped out, first to England and from there to Italy. He and Jane corresponded faithfully, and it was only once he was in Italy that she noticed that his tone had changed. He sounded discouraged, and alternated between fear and rage, and he couldn't tell her what he'd seen, so she could only guess how hard the war was for him. Both his parents died in the first year he was away, which upset him deeply too. There were long periods when she didn't hear from him at all, depending on where he was and if there was mail service. Then he would surface again. After he'd been in Italy for a few months, she noticed the tremor in his handwriting. The letters no longer sounded like him, and when he returned from the war in the summer of 1945, she could see why. He was a changed man. Amelia was five years old, didn't remember him, and cried each time she saw him or he tried to pick her up, which either made him cry, or storm out of the room, slamming the door behind him.

The doctors said he was suffering from shellshock and battle fatigue and it would heal in time, but it never did. He was thirty years old, and the death of his parents in a relatively short time after he left had added to his trauma. Once he came back, he no longer saw his old friends or went to his club. His job at the publishing house had been filled by a woman, who was doing an excellent job, for a lower salary than they'd paid him. She was a war widow now and they didn't want to upset her and let her go. The job market was flooded with young, healthy men looking for work, and Alfred was turned down for every job he applied for. It was clear that he hadn't recovered yet. He either flew into a rage over something they asked him, or, as at one interview, broke down in tears when they asked him about his war experience. Eventually he stopped going to interviews, and sat at home, brooding and drinking all day, while Jane struggled to find ways to cheer him up. His preference was gin, but he would drink anything he could lay hands on. Jane would throw away the bottles when she found where he concealed them, but he always had more hidden somewhere. Without a job and drinking heavily, and Jane not working either, Alfred went through much of the money his parents and grandparents had left him very quickly. He did some gambling at a private poker club, and a lot of drinking, and sat in a chair in a haze all day, lost in thought, staring into space. At night he usually fell asleep listening to the radio. His return was nothing like Jane had imagined it would be, with two kindred spirits finding each other again and picking up where they left off. Alfred never found his way back to that place. He was lost, never to be found again.

At thirty-four, four years after he returned from the war, he was driving to Connecticut to visit a friend from his army days that Jane had never heard of before when he drove off a cliff into a ravine and was killed. He didn't leave a note, so she was never sure if it was suicide or an accident because he was drunk. She suspected the former but could never prove it. He had been profoundly depressed for four years, with night sweats and nightmares almost every night, and he refused to get treatment for it. He insisted he was fine, but they both knew he wasn't.

Jane found herself a heartbroken widow at thirty-two. Her own parents had died by then, so she had no one to turn to for help when she discovered that Alfred had gone through almost all his money and had no life insurance. What he had left she put in an investment account with his military benefits, for Amelia's education and emergencies that might come up. Fortunately, he had purchased their apartment from his inheritance from his grandparents before the war, so she and Amelia had a roof over their heads, but very little more than that.

Amelia was nine when her father died, attending the Chapin School, an exclusive private girls' school on the East Side. Jane had attended Chapin too, and Amelia never suspected her mother's terror when she discovered Alfred's circumstances. They barely had enough to live on with the little that was left. Jane tried to get another magazine job and couldn't find one. She hadn't worked in nine years, and only had had a year's experience before that.

She finally found a job as a junior editor in a well-known publishing house, similar to Alfred's first job when she married him. She found she had a talent for editing, and young writers liked working with her, and she enjoyed encouraging them. Beyond that, she had a keen eye for manuscripts that were submitted that she was sure would be commercial successes, and she was often proven right. She had an uncanny knack for finding the proverbial needle in the haystack, discovering unknown authors whose novels became bestsellers. She rose quickly in the ranks of the publishing house she worked for, Axelrod and Baker. Phillip Parker, her boss, was impressed by her abilities, and she got regular promotions and raises. She learned to live frugally and provided everything Amelia needed. Within six years, she became the Assistant Publisher, and since her boss was nearing retirement, she had an eye on his position, and he hinted to her regularly that she was almost sure to get it. In fact, she had been doing his job more than he was for the past three years. He had frail health and he told her it was only a matter of time before she'd get his position as publisher. She worked hard in order to be worthy of it and took work home at night. She was doing the work of two people, his job and her own.

She was proud of the work she did and loved working with the authors. She knew many of them personally, made a point of getting to know the new ones, and continued encouraging young writers. It was rewarding work, and she made a decent salary. She'd had several offers from literary agencies to become an agent, which might have been more lucrative, but she was loyal to the house she worked for, and they paid her well. She was able to provide all the things Alfred would have if he hadn't blown most of his money before drinking himself to death. The autopsy had shown that he was drunk when he drove over the cliff. She had been angry at him for a long time afterwards but had finally made her peace with it. Alfred's death was due to the war. It wasn't his fault.

Neither Alfred nor Jane had grown up with extreme luxury. Their families' fortunes had dwindled, as had the fortunes of many aristocratic families after the Great Depression. But both their families were still comfortable before the war and had provided for their children. Jane and Alfred came from blue-blooded lineage, had been educated at the best schools and colleges, knew the right people, and lived on the edge of New York

Society, among people of their own kind. They had never been deprived growing up, and Jane was determined to see to it that her daughter lacked for nothing. She had sent her to one of the best private schools in the city too. Amelia had pretty dresses when she went to birthday parties. They were invited to the finest homes, and Amelia to the best parties. Jane was a member of the Colony Club, one of the most exclusive women's clubs in New York. And she saw to it that the girls Amelia met and made friends with were from the "right" families. The New York Social Register was Jane's bible, and she made sure that the people they socialized with were in it. Given her background, people who didn't know her well assumed she was a snob, but she wasn't. She was kind to everyone at work, but where Amelia was concerned, she wanted her to have the best opportunities, and tried to be sure that she grew up among the same kind of people her parents had grown up with. Jane never strayed far from that safe, familiar world, and didn't allow Amelia to do so either. When the time came, she wanted Amelia to marry someone from that world.

Giving Amelia the best of everything had been a fierce struggle for Jane. Her existence since Alfred's death had been a life-and-death battle to make ends meet, and she never wanted Amelia to go through that when she grew up.

Amelia never knew how often Jane deprived herself of a new coat or dress or hat or shoes, or even a new skirt for work, for her daughter's benefit. Jane was a pretty woman and she dressed up what she had with a bright scarf, or her mother's jewelry. She always wore her mother's pearls to work. She looked and sounded like what she was, a beautiful, ladylike, distinguished, aristocratic woman from an upper-class background, with an excellent education. She had been grooming Amelia all her life to appeal to the right man one day and to marry someone who would care for her and protect her and support her, so she would never have to make the sacrifices her mother had after Alfred's death. Jane was willing to sacrifice everything for her daughter.

Only a month before, on Christmas, Amelia had made her debut at the Infirmary Ball, one of the most exclusive debutante cotillions in New York, where Astors and Vanderbilts had made their debuts before her. Many of the girls Amelia had gone to school with had come out with her. She had worn a beautiful dress that they had picked out at Bergdorf Goodman. It was a simple heavy white satin gown by Pauline Trigère with a tiny waist that showed off Amelia's slim figure and a skirt shaped like a bell. Amelia was a beautiful girl, with a perfect body, long blond hair, and big blue eyes. She was a younger, almost exact replica of her mother. Jane was beautiful at forty-one, and they looked like sisters.

Amelia was exquisite coming down the stairs

with her escort, to curtsy as she was presented, under the crossed swords of the West Point cadets. Teddy Van Horn, a childhood friend, had been Amelia's escort, and he looked handsome in white tie and tails and was a year older than Amelia. She had no romantic interest in him whatsoever. They were just friends, which made the evening easier than if there had been romantic sparks between them. Jane had made her debut at the same ball twenty-three years before. And even now, at forty-one, she remembered how excited she had been. It had been the high point of her life until she married Alfred.

The beautiful dress had put a strain on Jane's budget, which she never discussed with Amelia. Alfred's remaining money, which she'd saved and invested, paid for college. Amelia's dorm room, everything that went with it, and her expenses were a stretch on Jane's current salary, but as soon as her boss retired and she got the position she'd been waiting for as Publisher, her finances wouldn't be quite so tight. She was looking forward to it and knew it would be soon.

Jane could manage in the meantime, just as she had for the past nine years. Amelia was eighteen now, and once she finished college and got through law school in seven years, Jane could heave a sigh of relief. They had made it this far, and she knew that she could hang on for another seven years of keeping a hawk eye on their budget, without Ame-

lia ever feeling the pinch of it or being deprived.
Jane would die before she would ever shortchange
Amelia and make her aware of her mother's struggle. She wanted Amelia to make a brilliant marriage, so she would never have to worry about
anything. She wanted her to marry for love of
course, but it was as easy to love a rich man as a
poor one. Amelia was well behaved, so Jane wasn't
worried about who she'd meet in college. She was
always in the library working to keep her grades
up, and she had done well so far. Jane was proud of
her. Amelia was a serious student with good morals
and values, and a kind heart. She would have been
devastated if she had known of her mother's strug-
gles to support her.

Jane had worn a plain black velvet evening
gown to Amelia's debut just before Christmas. She
had found it in a secondhand shop where wealthy
women often sold their cast-off clothes. It was by
Charles James, and she'd found a handsome short
mink Galanos jacket to go with it. She looked just
as elegant as all the other mothers at the cotillion
and was prettier than most of them. Amelia and
Jane were both beautiful women and looked well
in whatever they wore. Amelia's dress was one of
the most beautiful there.

Amelia had been pleased to be invited to the
cotillion and had expected to be. She and her
friends had talked about it with anticipation all
through high school. It didn't have deep meaning

for her the way it did for her mother and some of the other girls, but she knew it would be fun. It was a rite of passage into adulthood. She had chafed for a while about the origins and purpose of the cotillion in the past. Debutante balls were originally meant to introduce young women of good families to Society, with the intention of finding husbands for them. It had always been the case in the United States and Europe. But few young girls married at eighteen anymore, "fresh out of the schoolroom," as they used to say. Many or even most went to college now, and a number of them met their husbands there, as Jane pointed out when Amelia complained briefly about the cotillion being archaic. She was bothered too that anyone who was not from their white upper-class milieu was excluded. It seemed wrong to her.

"It's a cattle market, Mom," Amelia had grumbled briefly, "and all the cattle are just like us. Why is that okay?"

"It is *not* a cattle market. It's a night designed to make you feel like Cinderella, and if you meet your Prince Charming, then that's wonderful. It's a rite of passage for people like us, like a club, to show off our daughters we're so proud of. And you know all the girls coming out with you. You went to school with many of them." The others went to schools like Spence and Brearley, the rival schools to Chapin. Amelia had given up her reservations. She couldn't change the rules, even if she disapproved that all of the debutantes were white and Christian. The year before, Amelia had been deeply moved by the nine brave students who had been the first students to desegregate Central High in Little Rock, Arkansas. She had followed it closely on the news and took their situation very much to heart.

"It's not right, Mom, that they're not included too."

"No, it's not right," Jane agreed with her, "but history moves slowly. It will change one day, but most people in this country aren't ready for that to happen yet. One day integration will be the norm. The whole country isn't there yet."

"They need to hurry up. We're no better than they are."

"It will happen in your lifetime," Jane reassured her. "Probably by the time you're my age. Little Rock was a first big step toward that. But we can't fight everyone's battles, we can only fight our own, and that's not our battle to fight." Jane's struggle every day was to do the best she could for her daughter and support them both.

"Maybe it should be our fight too," Amelia had said earnestly, only a month before. The inequities of segregation had upset her since she was a young child. She hated the idea that some people were treated differently. And there was no question that events like debutante balls excluded many people and were only open to a select few. It was a very

exclusive club. The purpose of deb balls and presentations of marriageable young women hadn't
changed for centuries. It was an antiquated tradition, and a thinly veiled effort to find husbands for
young girls as they came of age.

In the end, despite her reservations, Amelia had
had fun, particularly since so many of her friends
from school were there, and she had stopped com-
plaining about it. She had fun with Teddy and the
many girls that were debs with her. She didn't consider it an earth-shattering event that would change
her life, but it was a fun party, and she loved her
dress.

As Jane sat down at her desk with the thick
cream-colored envelope with her name on it in elegant calligraphy, and a French stamp, indicating it
had been sent from Paris, a new door opened to
Amelia, beyond her mother's deepest hopes for her.
Jane read it carefully and smiled. In the presence of
the President of France and Ambassador Hervé Al-
phand, the French Ambassador to the United
States, with the Duchesse de Maillé and the Duc de
Brissac, as co-chairmen of the event, two hundred
and fifty French debutantes were to be presented
to Paris Society at a ball held for the first time at
the Palace of Versailles, and Miss Amelia Whitney
Alexander was on the list of forty American young
women who were included in the number of invi-
tees. It specified that the Americans had to have
been presented as debutantes in the U.S. in 1956

and '57, which was Amelia's case, having just come out in December 1957 a month before, and debutantes who would be presented later in the year in December 1958 were acceptable. Debutantes from earlier or later years were not included. And more specifically the girls had to be from seventeen to nineteen years of age. Jane's smile widened as she read down the list of the Honorary committee and the ball committee, which included several Bourbons, among them the pretender to the throne of France, if there were still a king. On the list were a number of royals, and Miss Mary Stuart Montague Price was General Chairman on the American side. And one could assume that almost all on the list of debutantes were from aristocratic families. The American debutantes whose names Jane recognized were from the most distinguished families in the country. It was not a list which reflected wealth or fame, but bloodlines and ancestry. And it was a great honor and compliment for Amelia to be invited.

Jane's mind raced immediately to what the event might cost her, in terms of plane tickets, the hotel, expenses while they were in Paris, and possibly another lighter, more summery dress than the heavy satin one Amelia had just worn to the cotillion. But there was no way that Jane would deprive her daughter of the experience if Amelia wanted to go. Jane intended to do everything she could to convince her if Amelia hesitated. She didn't speak

French and might feel shy about it. But it was a fantastic opportunity for any girl her age, to be presented at the Palace of Versailles, formerly the Court of Louis XIV. It would be an unforgettable event for her to experience, and an amazing opportunity for her to meet young men far beyond her usual circle of friends. She might marry a French prince, or an English duke, Jane fantasized. Her mind raced at the thought of all the advantages for Amelia that might come of it.

She vaguely remembered that the young Queen Elizabeth had recently stopped the presentation of debutantes at the Court of Saint James and declared it an antiquated tradition, so the French had risen to the occasion, and this would be the first Debutante Presentation at the Palace of Versailles. The ball was to be held on the twelfth of July. Jane carefully set the invitation down on her desk, to show Amelia when she got home. She was coming to spend the weekend with her mother, so the timing of the arrival of the invitation was perfect. The favor of a reply was requested by February first, from those who wished to participate. She hoped that Amelia would be as excited as she was. It was an honor to be chosen as one of the forty Americans being invited.

Jane read through the rest of her mail, made some notes of things she had to do, and looked out the window at Central Park in the dark. There was still snow on the ground, and she stood thinking about the ball as she heard Amelia's key turn in the lock. She bounded into the room in saddle shoes and a plaid skirt, a navy twin set, a pea coat with a white wool cap and mittens, and a face red from the cold. Her long blond hair hanging down her back made her look like Alice in Wonderland, as she walked into the living room and smiled at her mother. The two women looked strikingly alike. Jane went to hug her daughter and smiled happily to see her. It was the first week of school after the Christmas holidays, and Jane had missed Amelia once she went back to the dorm. They had spoken several times that week. They usually spoke every day. They were very close, enjoyed each other's company, and got on well.

"How was school?" Jane asked her as they sat down on the couch in the living room. The room wasn't large, but it was elegantly arranged, with antiques Jane had inherited from her family and Alfred's, and it had a warm, welcoming feeling to it. Amelia loved their apartment. It was just big enough for the two of them and felt cozy and inviting.

"Long," Amelia answered. "I already have three papers due. It feels like they're punishing us for having had a vacation." The cotillion already felt light-years away. "I have to work all weekend," she said, looking disappointed. She wanted to see her friends and go to a movie with her mother. They had promised to go on Sunday before Amelia went back to school. And there was a movie theater that was playing *Funny Face* with Audrey Hepburn and Fred Astaire, and they both wanted to see it.

"That's fine. I have some things to do too. This week was crazy in the office. We have several important books coming out in the next few months." Amelia had grown up with only her mother, so they were friends now as well as mother and daughter, and allies in most things. They rarely argued and both had easygoing personalities.

They chatted for a few minutes, and Jane couldn't hold back any longer. She walked to her leather-covered antique English desk that had been her father's, picked up the invitation, and walked back to the couch and handed it to Amelia.

"Look what came in the mail today," she said, unable to conceal her excitement. Amelia took it from her, read down the lists of all the names, and the explanatory cover letter, and looked up at her mother.

"Are they kidding? They're all princesses and countesses. Why would they want me there?"

"Because you have distinguished ancestors, and maybe they got the list from the Infirmary Ball. It sounds incredible. The first debutante presentation at the Palace of Versailles. That's so exciting." Amelia looked considerably less enthused than her mother.

"It sounds too fancy to me, and I don't speak

French. I knew most of the girls I came out with. I wouldn't know anyone there."

"You don't need to speak French. It's not a speaking part. You walk down the aisle or a staircase on the arm of your escort, you curtsy just like you did at the Infirmary Ball, and that's it, and you've made your debut in France too. At Versailles."

"I don't know any boys there to be my escort," Amelia said, trying to back out. It sounded intimidating to her. Most of the French debutantes had titles. Some were even princesses.

"Read the letter. They will supply a suitable escort for the debutantes coming from abroad. There will be five hundred escorts for two hundred and ninety girls. Amelia, you have to do it. You can't miss an opportunity like that. You'll have the memory of it forever."

"I already did it here, Mom. How many times do I have to be presented? It'll be the same thing all over again, with French subtitles." Amelia shrugged and handed the invitation back to her mother, unimpressed and unenthused about going.

"It's at Versailles. Nothing you've ever done will equal that," Jane insisted. She could already envision it, with Amelia looking like a princess too.

"Why do you want me to, Mom?" Amelia looked discouraged.

"Because when life gives you an opportunity

like that, I think you have to embrace it. And I'll be there with you. You won't be alone."

"It sounds scary to me."

"It's a chance to make friends in another country."

"And marry a duke or a prince, right?" Amelia teased her, but she knew she wasn't far from the truth. "I don't want to be Cinderella, Mom. I did the cotillion, that was enough. I didn't meet a handsome prince. I had fun. The whole concept is out of another century. I don't need to come out twice. Once was enough and I don't want a husband for about another ten years. I want to finish college and go to law school."

"You'll be too old to be a deb at Versailles by then. This is the year you're supposed to do it. After that you'll be a post-deb and they won't want you."

"This is 1958, Mom, not 1850. It's ridiculous."

"No, it's not. Consider it a fabulous costume party. You'll even meet some American girls, you can speak English to them."

"And what do I say to my escort after 'Bonnjoor,' when I have no idea what he's saying to me?"

"You give him that killer smile of yours and he'll melt at your feet." Amelia smiled at her mother's romantic illusions and faith in her, and then looked worried.

"Are you going to *make* me, Mom?" Amelia looked stubborn for a minute, and Jane could see that this wasn't going to be as easy as she'd thought. Amelia was sounding obstinate.

"I'm not going to *make* you do anything, but I am going to try to convince you. I think it's a fantastic opportunity, and I don't want you to miss it. I think you'll regret it forever if you don't go."

"No, *you* will," Amelia said pointedly. She knew her mother. She wanted the best of everything for her daughter, sometimes too much so.

"It's one night out of your life. How terrible could it be?" Jane wheedled, trying to sway her.

"It sounds boring, and pompous. They're probably all snobs. And it's expensive. The letter said there's a five-hundred-dollar fee if I do it. I'd rather have the money for new ski equipment. We have a long weekend coming up. I want to go to Vermont with friends from school." Amelia was athletic, which was often costly.

"You can rent the equipment, and five hundred dollars isn't a lot for an opportunity like this," but the rest of the expenses would be, Jane knew. She didn't care, she wanted Amelia to have the experience.

"I'll think about it." Amelia didn't want to argue with her mother about it, and she could see that Jane was determined. Jane nodded. She knew how rigid Amelia could be if she dug her heels in, and she didn't want her to refuse.

"We'll talk about it on Sunday," Jane said, with a determination Amelia knew only too well. When her mother wanted something badly enough, she was relentless, especially if it was for Amelia.

"I'll probably have my promotion by then, and a nice big fat raise," she reassured her, "and we can go on a little trip afterwards, in Provence or somewhere, just the two of us. It'll be fun." Amelia smiled. She could see a ball at the Palace of Versailles in her future, with a lot of stuck-up French people who didn't speak English and would probably snub her and be rude to her and consider her some kind of hick and treat her like a tourist, but once her mother got that look in her eye, wild horses would be easier to deal with. "Come on, let's go have dinner. Gloria left us a roast chicken. I'm starving," Jane said, and gave her daughter a hug.

"Me too," Amelia said. She put an arm around her mother's waist, and they walked to the kitchen together. Jane gave her a quick kiss, and started to organize dinner, and not another word was said about the ball at Versailles that night, but Amelia knew her mother wasn't going to forget it. It was beginning to seem unavoidable, and she would have to be presented as a deb, again. She felt like she was about to be auctioned off to the highest bidder, or a handsome prince, according to her mother.

The plan sounded stupid to Amelia, and she didn't want a husband, especially not a French one. It was all just too weird. She forgot about it after that and spent the weekend working on her papers.

Jane didn't mention it again until shortly before Amelia had to leave to go back to the dorm on Sunday. She wanted to go to the library after dinner.

Jane picked the invitation up from her desk and waved it at her. "And the ball at Versailles?" Amelia let out a terrifying groan.

"Oh God, why do I have to? Stop trying to marry me off, Mom."

"I'm not. I just want you to have fun." Jane looked determined, and Amelia knew she wouldn't win, so she might as well give in.

"Do I have a choice?" Amelia said, with a glance of resignation at her mother. She'd been hoping she would forget or give up.

"Actually," Jane smiled at her, "no, you don't. Trust me. It will be fabulous. You'll be glad you went. And we'll do something fun afterwards, a little trip in France."

"Okay, I give up," Amelia said, rolling her eyes, and went to get her bag. She was wearing jeans and saddle shoes, a heavy Irish sweater, and the pea coat.

"I'm sure you won't regret it," her mother promised.

"*Argghkkk.* You are the stubbornest person I know," Amelia said, exasperated.

"Thank you." Her mother smiled at her. "I love you too. And you'll thank me when you're a duchess with your own château."

"I think I hate you," Amelia said with a grin,

kissed her, and hurried out the door to go back to her dorm. July was so far away, it didn't seem real anyway.

Jane filled out the form that night, wrote the check, and mailed it from her office in the morning. She was absolutely certain that the ball at Versailles was going to be amazing, and Amelia was going to love it.